Secrets of Oscuros

THE PROTECTORS' PLEDGE

DISCARD

Danielle Y. C. McClean

CaribbeanReads Publishing

The Protectors' Pledge is the third place winner of the 2016 Burt Award for Caribbean Literature which recognizes three English-language literary works for young adults written by Caribbean authors. The Burt Award is the largest prize for Caribbean children's literature. It is sponsored by CODE and made possible by the generosity of William Burt and the Literary Prizes Foundation. NGC Bocas Lit Fest is a partner in the Burt Award for Caribbean Literature.

All rights reserved.
CaribbeanReads Publishing,
Basseterre, St. Kitts, West Indies
First Edition
ISBN: 978-0-9978900-7-5 Paperback
         978-0-9978900-8-2 Ebook
Library of Congress Control Number: 2017935656
Printed in the USA

For those whose imaginings are not yet reality and for those who help transform such dreams into certainties

ACKNOWLEDGEMENTS

This book would not have been possible without the support and love of my wonderful family and friends. Thank you to my mother, Rosemarie; my husband, Tino; Bernie, Mary and Rudy (Mom and Dad Cooper), Uncle Hermes, Lee, Aunt Hebe, Rae, and all you other marvellous persons in my life, for having read countless manuscript revisions, listened to endless chapter readings, and generously shared your insightful thoughts and advice. Your steadfast encouragement of my dreams is priceless, and you are each a true blessing to me.

To my father, Hector—my indefatigable champion—I look up, and thank you as well. You saw my strengths before I even knew that they were there, and fostered them with an unwavering pride. I miss you terribly.

I am also grateful to talents such as Paul Keens-Douglas, John Mendes, Rhona Baptiste, Dr. J. D. Elder, Dr. Gordon Rohlehr, Dr. Merle Hodge, and Gérard Besson—to name but a few—who, through their own words, celebrate and preserve the rich linguistic and cultural traditions of Trinidad and Tobago. Their literary works have been a tremendous source of enjoyment and inspiration over the years, and they help to keep my homeland close, regardless of where I am.

Finally, I offer my sincere appreciation to Jeff Tidwell for my author photo; Eileen Heyes, who worked her magic on a not-quite-where-it-needed-to-be manuscript;

the talented editors at CreateSpace; Lorena for the interior illustrations; Ryan James and Cherise Ward for the front and back cover illustrations; Carol Mitchell of CaribbeanReads Publishing for her priceless insight, critique, and superb editing skills; and to the NGC Bocas Lit Fest and CODE for their dedication to Caribbean literature.

Contents

Prologue

The prisoner was out of breath. The rumble of heavy boots hitting the ground as the officers pursued filled his ears, but he continued to run. There was no way he was giving up now. It had taken months to orchestrate this escape, and though he had harboured doubts, the plan had actually worked. A breakout in broad daylight was the last thing security had expected. He had managed to get past the gates, but his absence was discovered much sooner than he had hoped which led to the current chase through the bustling streets of Landing Town. He was close to success though. His pickup location was within view.

"Stop! Not another move!"

The warning came from close behind. Panicked, he shoved startled men and women, even children, aside. Although he barely saw the looks of fear on their faces, he realised that they not only recognised him but also knew exactly what he was capable of. Jumping off the pavement, he darted into the traffic and whipped his head left, then right. Horns blared and tyres screeched. *Where are they? They should have been here by now!*

"I said stop! Don't take another step!"

He glanced back. The officers now had weapons in hand. He was no fool and he knew they wouldn't hesitate to use deadly force. He stopped and turned. *This can't be how it all ends.* The officers were no longer running. They were approaching slowly, their guns pointing directly at his chest. *It's over.* Then, just as he began to raise his arms in surrender, a dark-green car raced into view, aiming straight for him. There was no time to react. A back door flew open, almost hitting him in the ribs. A pair of hands reached out and brusquely pulled him inside.

Onlookers ducked and scattered as officers shot at the fleeing vehicle, but the bullets did not stop the escape. The plan had worked. The fugitive was on his way to Oscuros.

Chapter 1

A Stranger Knocks

"JASON! Jason Felix Theodore Valentine!"

Granny B's call pierced its way from the kitchen, zipped along the narrow main corridor of the brick cottage, shot under the bedroom door, and found its mark on JV's well-attuned but less-than-receptive ears. He pulled the pillow down tighter over his head. Today was Saturday, and there wasn't one part of his body that was ready to leave the comfort of his sheets.

"JASON!"

1

He considered feigning sleep then thought better of getting on the wrong side of Granny B on the very first day of his much-anticipated two-month-long vacation. Groaning, he pushed aside the pillow, dragged himself up, and looked out of the window. It was early. Much too early. The trees of the Oscuros Forest were black against a sky still filled with inky blue and purple.

JV knew those trees well. From as far back as he could remember, he would accompany Granny B into Oscuros and amble around carrying her big old basket pretending to help search for bachelor's button, lantana, shining bush, or any of the many other herbs she collected. In reality, he mostly amused himself following lizards and frogs, and although there were times when he wandered out of Granny B's sight, he never ventured too far away.

Often he felt a strange pull from the forest—as if an unseen force wanted to usher him deeper in, away from his grandmother, his home, and his village. On those occasions he would resist the mysterious tug and stay where he could hear Granny B's low mutterings. He knew that she would be bending close to the ground, inspecting leaves, stems, and flowers, and assessing whether they would come in handy the following week. The curve of her bosse back, which had earned her the insolent but catchy nickname "Bosse B" among Alcavere's children, would be more pronounced as she bent over, and JV would question for the hundredth time why such a skilled healer hadn't fixed her own conspicuous imperfection. Her long-standing explanation that some things in life were beyond fixing had never been acceptable to him.

Studying the dark skyline, he wondered why he'd never gone exploring on his own. Granny B wouldn't have minded and he wasn't afraid of the ever-shifting shadows or intimidated by the way the Caribbean sun never fully reached the forest floor. And he certainly didn't believe all those stories about the Oscuros Forest being a haven for the soucouyant—an old crone who shed her skin at night, turned into a ball of fire, and drank human blood—or the shape-shifting lagahoo who prowled during the dark hours always ready to sink his fangs into his next victim. Those tall tales were for babies and JV was twelve, after all.

Yes, it was definitely time to embark on a quest. Although he had never met his parents, he liked to think that he had inherited his lust for adventure from them. His bedroom walls were lined with books filled with peril and excitement, and he had read and reread all the exploits of their brave young heroes. His dreams were drama-packed and danger-fraught escapades in which he scaled cliffs, dived for lost treasure on the ocean floor, and navigated jungles in search of forgotten cities. He was ready for live action, and it was waiting for him just beyond his backyard. This holiday for sure he was going to—

"JASON!"

All thoughts of Oscuros fled JV's brain.

"Coming!" he shouted, then mumbled, "And it's JV, Granny, not Jason." He fished his slippers from under the

3

bed, put them on, and followed the smell of freshly-made coconut bakes.

As he peered into the den of delights—JV's name for the kitchen—he was happy to see his grandmother transferring a steaming, flat, round loaf from a baking sheet to a cooling tray on the table. Her two grey braids were pinned in their usual place across the nape of her neck and a dish towel hung over her right shoulder, which was three inches lower than the left.

He stepped from behind the wall onto the slate-grey linoleum tiles and surveyed the small room. It was in its usual state of disorder: a measuring spoon was balanced precariously on the edge of a well-stacked sink; baking pans and trays of various sizes lay scattered along the counter tops; a pile of onion, garlic, and fruit skins waited to be tossed into the bin; and a fresh, fine layer of flour covered all visible surfaces.

A sharp metallic rattling drew his attention to the corner by the window. JV saw Granny B's parakeet, Kockot, using a clawed foot to drag an empty food tin along the bottom of her cage.

"All right, all right, Miss Lady," Granny B said. "Every morning you'll make noise so? You know I didn't forget you. Your breakfast is coming." She lifted the latch on the cage, carefully opened the door, and filled Kockot's dish with pieces of mango and banana. "When will you talk for me, eh?"

"Morning, Granny."

Granny B froze then leaned forward slightly. Kockot was still pecking at the fruit. Chuckling, Granny B shook her head, turned around, and glanced at JV.

"Oh, you're finally up, Jason?" She closed the cage. "Well, good thing."

She shuffled back to the stove, and JV inhaled the heavy scent of saltfish simmering with onions. Buljol was his favourite dish, and he kept his eyes on the pan as Granny B added the diced tomatoes and pepper.

"We have to make a trip to the market before it gets too late, eh," she said, mixing the contents and taking a taste. "You know how the freshest produce goes quick, quick. Well, come on. Help with the table. As good-looking as you are with those long lashes and dimples, it can't set itself, you know."

JV stifled a yawn and got out the place mats, all the while thinking of the countless other things he would rather do on the first morning of his vacation. Sleeping in was at the top of his list, of course, since the school term did not grant much time for lolling around in bed. Granny B always made sure that he was up by six thirty on a weekday; that he had something to eat, was show-ered, and was dressed in his well-starched uniform of khaki long pants and a monogrammed blue shirt; and that he was waiting on the front porch by seven fifteen at the very latest—to guarantee that he did not miss his ride to school with the Pearson children. It was beside the point that their father's white station wagon never pulled up to the gate before seven thirty. According to Granny B, good manners dictated that he be ready "early o'clock." Maybe he could have negotiated for more sleep if she were the one taking him to school, but her ancient Ford Cortina was now only capable of short weekly trips to the market.

And weekends weren't much better. In Granny B's world, the prime time to do outdoor chores was in the early morning before the sun got too hot. So the first thing on his agenda during these eight blissfully school-free weeks was to sleep as long and as late as he could get away with. His next priority would be exploring the forest.

He put down the plates, knives, and forks in their places on the table and considered the mission he was devising—an exploratory trek into Oscuros, his very own adventure. He chewed on his thumbnail. The mission could be even more fun if he took someone along. It would still be his expedition, of course, but having company wouldn't hurt. The question was, who? He deliberated as he got two mugs from the cupboard overhead—one for Granny B's orange-peel tea and the other for his cocoa. His best friend, Riaz, was an obvious choice and would make a perfect co-explorer, but he was spending the vacation with some cousins in the capital.

There was a knock at the door, and Kockot gave a startled flap of her emerald wings. JV looked at the clock. It was just after five thirty. *Who could be out there at this hour?* he thought. A louder, more urgent series of knocks made it clear that whoever it was wasn't going away. Granny B turned off the stove and went to the door.

"Yes?" she asked after she pulled it open.

A tall man was on the other side, leaning against the frame with his right arm cradled against his chest. Despite the darkness, JV could make out sunken eyes set in a broad, middle-aged, and unshaven face. The man was perspiring heavily and in obvious pain.

"You Miss B?" he asked through gritted teeth. "The healer?"

"Yes, son. Come in, come in." She put her hand gently on his shoulder to usher him forward, while eyeing the wound on his swollen forearm. "Snake got you? What kind?"

"Not sure. It was too quick."

"Well, first things first. Let's keep that arm nice and low." Granny B led the stranger into the kitchen. She put on the old-fashioned reading glasses that hung from a silver chain around her neck, pulled a chair away from the table, and motioned for him to sit. "JV, go get some twef while I clean off the bite. Make haste, now."

"Yes, Granny."

JV bolted out the door, raced across the front porch, and jumped down the two concrete steps that led into the yard. Orange streaks now slashed through the sky's ever-lightening purples and blues. He ran past the hibiscus shrubs and the crotons along the side of the house and past Granny B's old car resting comfortably in its usual spot under the soursop tree. He flashed by the guava, avocado, and orange trees and stopped only when he had reached the wire fence almost completely covered with a slender, brilliantly green vine. With its reputation as a ward against bewitchment, twef was a common sight in villages such as Alcavere where there was still a healthy respect for superstition. JV pulled fistfuls of the shiny three-pronged leaves off the vine and dashed back to the house.

When he rushed in, Granny B was dipping a cloth in soapy water and gently applying it to the man's wound. She patted it dry and took a closer look at the bite marks.

"See the pattern here, Mr...."

"Phipps."

"Mr. Phipps. You see this pattern here?" she asked, pointing at the horseshoe-shaped impression of small cuts. "It wasn't a venomous one that got you. You're lucky, but you'll have to watch for infection."

The stranger closed his eyes and sighed.

Granny B studied him carefully. "I've been living in Alcavere since Moses parted the Red Sea, and I never saw you before," she said. "How did you know I could help?"

"Nah, I'm not from around here. Just passing through. I'm on my way up north and stopped to camp out not too far from here last night. Then this happened." He nodded toward his arm. "I didn't know what snake it was and thought the worst, so I started off for the village. Saw some folks who looked like they were heading to market. They told me about you and pointed the way."

Granny B looked across the kitchen and saw JV. He was still panting heavily but proudly held out his fists full of leaves, happy to have been of use in such a dire situation.

"You sure you left any leaves on the vine, Jason?" She smiled. "I just need a few to ease the pain. Rest the others on the far side of the counter over there for me, and I'll put them in the herb room later. And could you get a glass of water for Mr. Phipps, please?"

She put four or five leaves in her granite mortar, picked up the pestle, and began to pound away rhythmically, the cadence like the beat of a tribal war drum: POC, poc, poc, poc…POC, poc, poc, poc…POC, poc, poc, poc. So it went for a few minutes. Then Granny added a drop or two of a sweet-smelling oil, a little pinch of this and a little pinch of that, and finally pounded some more until the contents had reached the desired consistency. JV loved to watch his grandmother work. She followed no recipe that he could see, but her fingers always knew exactly what to do.

As JV looked on, Granny B used a wooden spatula to smear the thick green salve on the wound. She then took a piece of gauze from one of the kitchen drawers that served as their first-aid kit, cut off a generous square, and bandaged the man's arm tightly.

The soothing effect of the poultice was immediately visible. Mr. Phipps's shoulders dropped an inch, his face relaxed, and the lines on his deeply creased forehead became less pronounced. He slowly let out a long breath and opened his eyes, which he'd been holding tightly shut. Granny B patted his hand.

"When you knocked, we were just going to have breakfast, Mr. Phipps. It's not much—some coconut bake, buljol, and tea—but you can join us."

JV's eyes darted to the coconut bake, still untouched on the table. He wasn't sure he liked where things were heading. It was one thing to save a stranger's life but quite another to give an open invitation to breakfast, especially when bake and buljol were involved. He held his breath, waiting for Mr. Phipps's reply.

"Well, if it isn't too much trouble, Miss B, yes. I'd be grateful to have a little breakfast."

JV looked sorrowfully at the bake and buljol and mourned the loss of a potential third serving while Mr. Phipps moved to an unset place at the table.

"I really didn't eat much in the forest last night," he said.

JV snapped out of his woe and stared at the stranger. "You're staying in the forest?" he blurted. "I'll be exploring Oscuros this vacation!" He headed to the cupboard and pulled out another plate and mug, his displeasure at having to share his breakfast forgotten. "I kind of already know my way around certain parts 'cause I've been going in with Granny for a long time to help her collect herbs and stuff, but I really want to go exploring, you know? Maybe discover something cool or even a spot that no one else has ever seen. Have you been in Oscuros long? Have you seen anything interesting? Maybe I can go back with you?" JV was so excited that the mug almost slipped from his hand.

The sudden questioning seemed to take Mr. Phipps by surprise. He was staring at JV in a wide-eyed and open-mouthed sort of way when Granny B interrupted.

"Mind your manners, Jason. Mr. Phipps here didn't say yes to breakfast so he could go through an Alcavere version of the Spanish Inquisition, you know. Boy, let the man eat in peace."

JV sat down but eyed Mr. Phipps expectantly. The gentleman, however, did not seem to be in any rush to continue the conversation and helped himself to two slices of bake and a generous serving of buljol. After he had finished the first slice and sighed appreciatively, he said, "I wouldn't worry too much about that forest, you know, boy. I'm sure your granny here doesn't need you to go and get yourself lost."

JV's anticipation instantly turned to indignation.

"Lost? Who, me? No way! I couldn't get lost in Oscuros. Right, Granny?" He turned to his grandmother.

Granny B put a third spoonful of sugar in her tea, stirred, and smiled. "I don't think there's too much in Oscuros that Jason can't handle. And in any case," she added, looking at JV with an arched eyebrow, "he knows not to go beyond a certain point or to let sunset catch him in there." She took a sip of her tea and once again reached for the sugar bowl.

Not quite sure whether Granny B had provided suffi-cient support for his argument, JV pressed the matter further, between mouthfuls of bake. "I'm pretty good in the forest, you know. I don't need a compass to tell what

11

direction I'm going in, I know what plants to stay away from, and I can recognize lots of bird calls." He put the last forkful of buljol in his mouth and sat back, content with his breakfast and his list of skills.

Mr. Phipps studied him for a moment. "And what about the spirits? I'm no expert, eh, but you see that forest?" he said, pointing in the direction of Oscuros, "After only one night in there I can tell you it has spirits for sure. Don't ask me what type—it was dark and I couldn't see too good— but I could tell you plenty stories about the spirits in the forests down south. Make you think twice about heading in this one again."

JV lowered his eyes. *Oh great,* he thought. *Someone else trying to frighten me with superstitious nonsense.*

All the villagers ever seemed to talk about was spirits and supernatural creatures in the forest. He had heard many stories about Papa Bois and Mama D'Lo—the legendary guardians of Oscuros and fierce protectors of its flora and fauna. Then there was the story about a local arsonist who had entered the forest intent on setting a fire. According to village lore, the firebug's encounter with the guardians was so horrific that he never struck a match again and went to his grave without revealing the details of what had happened beneath those trees. JV didn't think that there was any truth to such tales, but he had begun to wonder if so many people, including this traveller, could be wrong. He bit his lip and Mr. Phipps snickered.

Granny B looked up from her tea, raised an eyebrow, and held Mr. Phipps's gaze. "Like I said, there's not too much in Oscuros that Jason can't handle."

The visitor smirked, shrugged, and took a third slice of bake along with another helping of buljol. Irked by how the conversation had gone, JV redirected his irritation to the quantity of food being consumed by their guest.

"You sure that it's only last night you didn't eat well?"

He didn't need to see Granny B's face to know that she was giving him a sharp look. One just did not speak to a guest or an adult like that in Granny B's house. JV watched as Mr. Phipps continued chewing steadily, apparently oblivious to the exasperation that he had caused.

"My goodness, look at the time," Granny B said as she drained her mug, stood up and started clearing away the empty dishes. "A quarter after six. Oh no, please don't rush yourself, Mr. Phipps. JV and I have to go to market for a few things, but you should rest a little before you head back out. We have a couch in there if you want to take a nap." She pointed to the modest sitting room just beyond the kitchen.

"Thank you, Miss B. I appreciate the hospitality."

"Jason, we're leaving in five minutes."

JV excused himself from the table and headed down the hallway to his bedroom. Halfway there, he turned, tiptoed back to the kitchen and stayed behind the wall.

"Quite a little man you have there," Mr. Phipps was saying.

13

"A good boy but stubborn like a mule and hot-foot too, as you can tell. Can't keep him home at all, at all. He's always after some adventure. Anyhow, you'll be all right until we get back?"

"Yes, ma'am. Don't worry about me. I'll be fine."

JV heard the scraping of chairs and crept away. He was already waiting outside his room when Granny B appeared in the hall. He waved her over.

"Granny, you sure you want to leave him here alone? Don't you think it's strange he's staying in the forest? He could be a thief," he whispered. "I don't mind staying and keeping an eye on him."

Granny B shook her head and smiled. "Jason, I've been around since Jesus was a boy, you know. What you really want is to get out of a trip to the market and to bother that poor man some more about the forest."

Unwilling to give up so easily, JV played his last card.

"But what if he steals something while we're gone?"

"Remember, Jason: 'Who sick does look for doctor.' Mr. Phipps was in trouble and came for help. But even if he's up to mischief, what could he really take?" Granny B chuckled. "If you think we have something in this house to steal, you better let me in on the secret." She stopped laughing and smiled kindly at him. "Don't forget the saying, son. 'One day for police and one day for thief.' Life always has a way of balancing things out in the end."

Resigned that he had lost yet another argument for the morning, JV nodded and sighed.

"OK. I'll get the basket, Granny."

Chapter 2

To Market, to Market

"Fresh fish! Fresh fish! Shark, carite, king. Fresh fish!"

"Get your provisions here! Cassava an' sweet potato. Eddoes an' yam."

Vendors' shouts rang out over the noisy buzz that came from all quarters of the market. Granny B picked her way through the crowds, stopping every few paces to examine the wares being sold and to say good morning to neighbours and friends. With basket in hand, JV hung back a few paces and took in all the sights and smells of the Alcavere marketplace. He would never openly admit to

15

enjoying these weekly trips with his grandmother, but the truth was that once in the midst of all the action, he found it quite entertaining.

On their left, JV spotted old Mr. Chin and his son Patrick at their fish stall. Mr. Chin was chatting animatedly with four customers, his razor-sharp knife either a barely visible blur as he adeptly cut the chosen fish into fillets or a glinting flash of metal when he wielded it in concert with his wild gesticulations. Patrick, in contrast to his father, worked silently, carefully arranging the display of fish and shrimp and intermittently sprinkling it all with water to keep everything fresh and the flies at bay. From where he stood, JV couldn't see the contents of the weather-beaten barrel beside the counter but knew it must contain throbbing mounds of legs and powerful, vice-like gundies—what with each blue crab trying to scramble to the top on its neighbours' backs. He wondered idly if any of them would ever make a successful break for freedom or if they were destined to keep pulling each other down.

"Jason, you still with me?" Granny B asked, glancing over her shoulder.

"Yes, Granny."

"Well, keep close," she said as she added a jar of honey and a half-pound bag of pigeon peas to the basket. "We're heading for the provisions right now."

JV knew only too well that Granny B's "right now" never turned out to be as immediate as it sounded. In fact, they had only gone a few paces when Doris George, who was bargaining with a weary-looking Mr. Charles over the price of a hand of bananas at the fruit stall, caught sight of them and instantly put her haggling, as well as the bananas, on hold. As Doris turned to hail Granny B, Mr. Charles looked up to the heavens and mouthed what appeared to be a short prayer.

"Miss B! Miss B! Wait a minute." Doris's voice thundered over the general clamour of the market. "Doh worry, Charles. Ah comin' right back."

She charged through the crowd, her oversized yellow bag held above her head and a right elbow jutting out stiffly at her side, a good excuse for those who saw her coming to get out of the way.

JV groaned inwardly. Everyone in Alcavere knew Doris George. And Doris? She knew everyone's business, not only in Alcavere, but in any town within a twenty-mile radius, and for some reason, Granny B was her favourite audience. Perhaps Doris thought that because Granny B treated a number of villagers with various afflictions, the old lady was a good source for gossip. But since Granny B was not interested in salacious tattling and always said, in fact, that it was better to mind old clothes than people's business, JV knew that she tried to keep her interactions with Doris as infrequent and as brief as possible, however challenging that goal proved.

But alas, Doris was now upon them. As usual, her hair was hidden under a head wrap, and today's saffron-yellow print must have been specially selected to match her bag. Salt-and-pepper strands poked out just in front of her

17

ears, which were adorned with large gold hoop earrings that shone in the sunlight.

"Good mornin', Miss B. Ah knew ah would see you here today. Ah was jus' tellin' Charles to keep a lookout for you. You don't see how his bananas lookin'? And ah never in all my life see small oranges like the ones he tryin' to pass off. All the lettuce by De Couteau stall shrivel up. Everything in the market lookin' qualebay, qualebay. Mus' be the weather. We're supposed to be in rainy season but not a drop. All this heat has me tired! But anyhow, ah wanted to tell you thanks for that tonic you made for me." Doris gave her stomach a few contented pats. "Everything workin' good, good now."

"I'm so glad the sapodilla bark worked, Doris," Granny B said. "Oh my. That's the time? Come on, Jason, we have to get those provisions before—"

"But wait! Jason, you here too? Ah didn't even see you. Helpin' your granny out in the market? Nice child. So school on vacation now, eh? What you doin' for the holidays? Ah know you young people always gettin' into some kinda mischief, so your granny goin' to have to keep a good eye on you. Not so, Miss B?"

"Yes, of course, Doris, but Jason and I really have to—"

"And talkin' about mischief, just yesterday the Simon boy and some of his little ragamuffin friends went up old Pa Gregory's hog plum tree and started eatin' all the man's ripe plums. And what you think happen' when he came outside with a big stick to get them down? They pelt him with green plums and seeds. It's true the old man is a cantankerous so-an'-so—and ah even hear he dabblin' in obeah—but how those boys harass that man is criminal, ah tell you."

JV stifled a laugh. Randall Simon and his buddies had made a name for themselves as the village trouble-makers and had boldly chosen the imposing tree in front of Pa Gregory's house as their main liming spot. Confrontations between them and the old man were frequent, but this was the first time that JV had heard of one that involved a stick and flying plum seeds. He felt badly for Pa Gregory, but would have loved to have witnessed such a scene.

Doris pulled a handkerchief from the top of her dress and energetically mopped her brow. "And speakin' of criminals, you didn't hear how that big-time murderer, Tricky Dixon, escaped from prison in the capital yesterday? Yes, girl. Big search goin' on up there now. It's a good thing Alcavere not close to Landing Town or ah woulda been outta here so fas' you couldn't catch me for dust. But ah think we safe. Who would want to come and hide here anyway? Steups. This place so small that if you sneeze, all of Alcavere will say 'bless you.' Nah, ah think Tricky's still right there in the capital."

Doris kept up her monologue, and between the drone of her voice and the pleasant warmth of the morning sun, JV's mind was soon wandering again: first to how much fun it would be if he were up there in the capital with Riaz so that they could start their own investigation into Tricky Dixon's whereabouts (an inquiry that would undoubtedly result in Tricky's recapture as well as a reward and

19

limitless praise for himself and Riaz) and then to how he still needed to find a fellow explorer for his mission into Oscuros. Of course, this train of thought only led right back to a certain Mr. Phipps, whom he still knew very little about. And the more he pondered it, the greater his desire became to get some answers out of their house-guest once they returned home. There was no way JV was going to let him off the hook so easily a second time.

An unnaturally loud cackle from Doris, the pitch of which drew stares and a startled jump from those standing close by, brought JV out of his imaginings.

"But Miss B, ah really have to get going now. Look at the hour. Ah don't know how you always end up holdin' me in these long talks, eh, but ah still have to pass back by Charles and sort him and those bananas out before the scamp packs up and leaves for the day. Don't worry, though, you'll see me later. Ah'll pass by the house to get some tonic for that other thing ah was tellin' you about."

A conspiratorial wink, another cackle, and Doris George headed in the direction of poor Mr. Charles, who did indeed seem to be trying to make a quick escape.

The not-so-brief interlude with Doris safely behind them, Granny B and JV resumed their progression through the market. Straight ahead was the De Couteau provisions stall, which was to be their next and, if left to JV, final stop. The day was getting hot, the basket that he had been dutifully lugging around was beginning to feel like a leaden weight on his arm, and he was anxious to return home. His growing discomfort was at least partially relieved, however, when a few more paces brought them before rows of lettuce, carrots, peppers, yams, plantains, eddoes, cassava, and corn. They were neatly laid out on wooden counters at the front of the stall—colourful yes, but not exactly vibrant. JV eyed three empty plastic soft-drink crates stacked close to the hot peppers at one end of a counter and promptly took a seat, resting the basket on the ground beside him.

He looked on as Granny B walked along the rows of vege-tables. She picked up some plantains and gave them a gentle squeeze; closed her eyes and raised ears of corn to her slightly flared nostrils to assess their delicate scent; and peered intently at the heads of lettuce, perhaps to judge for herself whether Doris's analysis had been correct. For once, Doris had not exaggerated. JV knew from years of listening to Granny B that the sagging yellow-green lettuce leaves, their rippled edges tinged with a brown that, from all appearances, would continue its slow creep toward the centre, were evidence enough that the dry season had gone on too long and the rains were due.

Paulette De Couteau, noticing Granny B's prolonged interest in the lettuce, came up and smiled faintly from the other side of the counter. She was of medium build, probably in her forties, and her amber eyes reminded JV of stars, although he had not seen them twinkle for some time.

"All this sun and no rain really making things tough," she said, waving an arm apologetically over the wilting leaves.

Granny B nodded. "Well, we should have some rain soon, God willing." She selected a lettuce head that was not as bad as some of its neighbours and held it out to Paulette's son, Mason. "Here, Mr. Handsome. Come and weigh this for me, please."

Mason approached, said good morning to Granny B, gave a brief nod to JV, and took the lettuce. JV knew him from school. He was three grades ahead and was usually among a group of students who were to be found on the soccer field before classes began in the mornings, at break, during lunch, and immediately after the final bell at three o'clock. JV and some of his friends often looked on as one of the players ran the length of the field tapping the ball between one foot and the other, blocking an opponent who approached for a steal, or passing it off to a teammate. From the sidelines, JV would roar just as loudly and with as much enthusiasm as any of the players when the blur of white and black eluded the goalie and slammed into the net. Although the older students were friendly enough and JV longed to join in, neither he nor his friends had ever been invited to play, and he had always been too shy to ask.

"Perhaps next term," JV said to himself, averting his gaze from Mason's face and looking down to kick at the hard dirt with his leather sandals. He knew full well that even the eight weeks that stretched ahead would not be enough time for him to develop the necessary nerve.

Refocusing on the exchange between Granny B and Mrs. De Couteau, JV gathered that the conversation had shifted from the weather to Adelle, Mason's eight-year-old sister. Despite her young age, she was a fixture at the De Couteau stall on weekends, helping customers choose their produce and bagging their purchases. If she was not chatting with shoppers, she was tiptoeing on a stool at the back of the stall to reach a makeshift blackboard, carefully writing prices in coloured chalk and decorating the borders with flowers and hearts. JV had noticed that she and Mason seemed close and that her big brother called her Little Bird. He didn't see her at the stall that day.

"She's in punishment this weekend," Mrs. De Couteau was saying to Granny B.

"That sweet child?" Granny B asked. "What's she done?"

"Well, little madam left the house yesterday evening and didn't say boo to anyone about where she was going. You believe that? At eight years old? Nah, man, Miss B! As they say, we're 'taking in front' with this one. You have to bend de tree before it start to grow. If not, can you imagine what she'll be doing when she's thirteen and figures she's a grown woman?" Mrs. De Couteau let out an exasperated sigh.

"And the thing is that she doesn't usually give any trouble at all. Always playing quiet in her room with her dolls, making puzzles, helping her father, or two steps behind Mason. But yesterday...like she caught a vapse and just disappeared after dinner. We thought she followed Mason to football, and I was about to pass by the field when she came home." Mrs. De Couteau sucked her teeth and continued.

"Miss B, no amount of talking, threatening, or pleading would make that girl tell me where she went. I told her it was dangerous, that she has to always tell her father or me when she's leaving the house. And do you know what the little imp did? No quarrelling or backchat from her, you know. No, siree. She just nodded and went right off to her room. Earl was beside himself with worry…and it's the last thing he needs right now, in his condition." She looked off into the distance, over the drooping vegetables and up into the sun-baked hills, before continuing in a softer tone. "I wonder if it's because Mason is heading off to the city today?"

Mason, who was still fiddling with the lone lettuce and the scales, finally looked up.

"Don't worry too much, Mummy. You know Little Bird. She probably found a sick animal or something and is taking care of it in secret. I promise I'll talk to her before I leave."

Mrs. De Couteau relaxed slightly and gave her son a wan smile that didn't reach her eyes.

"Here's your lettuce, Miss B," Mason added. He handed it over and was soon on the opposite side of the stall, talking to other customers.

Jumping off the crates and dusting the seat of his pants, JV took the lettuce from Granny B and dropped it in his basket. Not too far away, he had heard the familiar call of Miss Jean, the sweets vendor, and he was hoping that he could at least buy a tamarind ball before they returned home. Or perhaps a piece of fudge or peppermint candy.

"So what's this about Mason heading to Landing Town?" Granny B asked Mrs. De Couteau as she rooted around in her shoulder bag for her purse.

"He's leaving this evening. You know how he is with his hands, right? If he's not off playing football, he's always tinkering with something or other. Well, he's serious about becoming a mechanical engineer and found an apprenticeship in the capital for a month. All this Tricky Dixon business going on up there has me a little worried, but it'll be good for him, I think. He'll get some experience and be able to make the kind of money he can't down here. It should also help us pay for his father's medications."

JV thought about how lucky Mason was to be going to Landing Town and to be travelling there by himself. JV had never been in a maxi taxi. According to Granny B, the large striped passenger vans "drove too fast and made the whole world deaf with their loud music," which made him doubt that he would ever be allowed to set foot in one of them, much less do so without his grandmother.

Having finally found her change purse, Granny B handed Mrs. De Couteau the money for the lettuce. JV decided this was as good a time as any to delicately bring up the topic of Miss Jean and her sweets.

"Um…Granny?" he tested hopefully.

"And how is Earl feeling?" Granny B asked Mrs. De Couteau. "I haven't seen him at the stall for two weeks now."

"Well, he has his good days and his bad ones," she responded. "This problem with Adelle didn't help, of course, but the doctor has him on some new tablets, so we're hoping for the best. Every week it's something else." She let out another weary sigh.

"You know you just have to say the word, and I can mix something up quick, quick for him that might help," Granny B offered.

Paulette twisted one of the gold rings on her fingers and shook her head slowly. "Thank you, Miss B, but we've never been ones for traditional medicine. No offense."

Granny B patted the younger woman's arm. "Just let me know if there is anything I can do to help." Then she looked across at JV. "But Jason, like you need to use the bathroom, or what? How you dancing, dancing so?"

"No, Granny. I just wanted to know if I can head over to Miss Jean now."

"Yes, yes. And take this with you." Granny B rummaged for her change purse once again. She pulled out two crumpled dollar bills and pressed them into JV's palm. "You could leave the basket, son. I may pick up one or two more things before I come to meet you."

He needed to hear no more. With a "Thanks, Granny," shouted over his shoulder, he scampered off toward the round old lady whose dimpled cheeks were as smooth and dark as the molasses candy that she sold.

When JV got to Miss Jean, she was already surrounded by a swarm of children, each vying for her attention, their arms waving dollar bills and loose fists jingling change. Seated on a little wooden stool in the midst of them all, she was indeed the Pied Piper of Alcavere. Four large wicker baskets lay at her feet, each exposing its goodies.

JV joined the throng and squeezed himself forward. He could see the array of treats now: bright-green papaw balls; red-and-white peppermint sticks, three to a pack; creamy squares of vanilla and chocolate fudge; perfectly round tamarind balls whose sugary coatings belied their tangy interior…and those were just the ones at the top. He knew that somewhere in there were also milky coconut drops and stick-to-the-roof-of-your-mouth, almost-black-with-molasses balls of toolum.

JV was so engrossed in his thoughts of getting to the candy that a sudden surge in the crowd knocked him off balance. He was only able to regain his footing by leaning heavily on a pair of narrow shoulders in front of him. The person spun around.

"What the…" But recognition instantly dawned on the vexed face, and its features softened into a big smile. "Hey, JV! You're lucky it's you. I was about to give whoever it was a good piece of my mind. How're you doing?"

It was Carol Pearson, his classmate and fellow passenger on trips to and from school in her father's car. Although they were the same age, Carol always seemed older to JV. He chalked it up to the fact that she, like most of the other children in his class, was a few inches taller than he was—that and the fact that she was always correcting him.

"I'm good, Carol. Just happy we don't have school for eight weeks. Oh, and sorry about pushing you. I was about to fall and—"

She waved him off. "Don't worry. No harm done." Her fingers found a few loose, curly strands of hair and poked them into the bun on top her head. "Hey, what do you want from Miss Jean?" she asked, eyeing JV's bills. "Give me your money and I'll get it. Just keep an eye on Pascal back there for me."

JV handed over the two dollars and put in his order for tamarind balls and fudge. He noticed Pascal, Carol's seven-year-old brother, at the edge of the crowd and eased his way out of the crush of bodies to stand next to him. Pascal was a precocious, plump little boy who didn't let his two missing front teeth and consequent lisp hinder his chatty enthusiasm.

"Hiya, JV. Carol'th getting your thweetths too? I'm getting peppermint thtickth. They're my favourite! What'th yourth?"

"Tamarind balls, but I'm also getting some fudge for my granny. She loves sweet stuff. You believe she puts sugar and condensed milk in her tea? So are you and Carol doing anything fun for the vacation?"

Pascal cocked his head and tapped an index finger on his chin. "Hmm...I don't think tho. But Daddy thayth he'll teach me to thwim, tho maybe we'll go to the beach. What about you? What are you going to do?"

JV was itching to tell him about his plans involving the forest but wasn't sure if he should. Most children in Alcavere didn't want anything to do with Oscuros, and JV knew that his eagerness to charge in there on an exploratory mission would probably seem strange. But that wasn't his only reason to hesitate. There was also the possibility his plans would be too well received and he could lose control over the adventure—a far more unsettling thought. He was still debating when Carol emerged with the goodies.

"Here you go, JV," she said, handing over the two packets of fudge and tamarind balls. "And here are your sticks, Pascal. Remember, Mummy said you can only eat one now."

"Yeth, yeth," the younger Pearson responded impatiently, ripping open the top of the plastic pack and hungrily starting on his first stick. Carol rolled her eyes and shook her head, then turned her attention back to JV.

"Got any plans for the rest of the day?"

JV had made up his mind. He realised that Carol might actually be a good second-in-command. She was smart and probably as adventurous as he was. He just hoped that she wouldn't try to pull too much of her know-it-all stuff. "Actually, yes. I'm going to start exploring Oscuros this afternoon. Want to come?"

"Sounds good to me," Carol said. "What're you looking for in there, anyway?"

"Nothing specific, but who knows what we'll find," JV answered, getting excited.

She shrugged. "OK, whatever. But Pascal will probably have to come with us."

The two classmates had barely begun to discuss their plans when JV was suddenly aware of a whisper emanating from the knot of children close by. His body immediately stiffened in trained response to the anger he felt at hearing the singsong:

> "Bosse B, Bosse B,
> Curled over like the letter C.
> Bosse B, Bosse B,
> If I run you never catchin' me!"

He saw that Granny B was making her way toward him. JV wished that the silly chant didn't bother him so much or that he could tell them to stop singing it, but he recognised the unlikelihood of either of those two things ever coming to pass. It was time to go.

"So see you around two, then?" he confirmed with Carol. "By the track to the forest."

She gave him a thumbs-up, and skipping his good-byes, JV left her, Pascal, and the barely audible singing behind as he ran off to meet Granny B.

Chapter 3

Beyond the Breadfruit Tree

It was close to two thirty before JV left for the forest. He knew that Carol was going to kill him, if she was still waiting around to do it. On the way home from the market, Granny B had mentioned a few chores that needed to be done. Some he had put off for weeks (like cleaning his room) and others she slipped in while he nibbled on tamarind balls. Watering the numerous potted and hanging plants along the front porch and helping her turn the kitchen from its current state of chaos into a gleaming, spotless space fell into this latter category.

To make matters worse, on arriving home they discovered that Mr. Phipps was gone, and with him, what was left of the bake and buljol as well as JV's chances of getting useful information about the forest. JV wasn't too sure what made him angrier: the missing leftovers or his lost opportunity with Mr. Phipps. Well, at least he finally had two people to go exploring with…if they were still there.

Hurrying along, he was almost at the track that would lead to Carol, Pascal, and the forest beyond when he spied a familiar yellow head wrap. Doris was heading toward Granny B's house. If he didn't think fast, she'd see him and bring an end to any plans he had for the afternoon. Ducking behind a tree, JV squeezed his eyes shut and held his breath. He counted to thirty and tentatively opened one eyelid. The coast was clear. Lickety-split, he dashed to the track, his fingers crossed that Carol and Pascal hadn't given up and gone home.

On turning at the next bend, he was happy to see that his fears were unfounded. Pascal, wearing a light-blue long-sleeved shirt and jeans, sat on a tree stump swinging his legs. Given how hot the day was, JV bet that it wouldn't be long before the younger Pearson's sleeves and pant legs were rolled up. Carol, who was similarly dressed except that her shirt was yellow, paced behind Pascal, a scowl on her face. Seeing JV, she stopped abruptly and launched into a reprimand.

"JV, you know how long we've been waiting here for you?" she asked, arms folded across her chest and her left foot tapping the ground.

JV bent over, hands on knees, and tried to catch his breath.

"Sorry I'm late," he panted. "Got held up at home. Thanks for waiting, though."

"Well, let's get going, then," Carol huffed. "Pascal and I have to be back home by four."

She started up the track without looking back. JV hoped that this was not a sign of how the rest of the afternoon would turn out. Hopping off his perch, Pascal skipped ahead to catch up with his sister, and JV, still breathing heavily from his sprint, followed.

As the three adventurers marched on, the dirt track became less pronounced until it was completely lost beneath a thick carpet of leaves and brush. Expansive boughs hung overhead, the sunlight filtering between their smaller branches to create mottled golden-brown patterns on the forest floor. All was still but for the crunch of dry leaves and twigs under the feet of Carol, Pascal, and JV. It was as though the unforgiving heat over the past seven months had drained the forest of any life.

Deeper in they went. The forest became denser, making it impossible for JV to use the sun to gauge time. They proceeded in relative silence until Pascal broke the peace.

"Tho, what'th it like living with Bothe B, JV?"

JV felt his pulse quicken.

"Pascal!" Carol hissed, giving her brother a hard look. "Bosse B is not her name. It's Miss B!" She shot JV a quick, apologetic look. Undaunted, Pascal forged ahead.

"Well, what'th it like living with Mith B, then?"

"What do you mean?" JV countered.

"Well, you know. Everyone callth her an obeah woman. People even think she'th ready for the madhouthe."

Carol pursed her lips, crossed her arms, and glared at Pascal. But JV had already heard all the rumours. Granny B, who knew so much about herbs and plants, was generally respected as a skilled healer, but there were those in the village who believed her to be some sort of witch and ordered their children to keep a respectful distance, and others who were convinced that she was "a little off".

"No, my granny doesn't deal in obeah, Pascal, and she isn't mad. She just knows a lot about nature and stuff. She's like a doctor...a doctor who makes her own medicine from plants." JV was pleased with his calm answer.

"Oh." Pascal thought for a minute, and then his finger went up to his chin and began tapping. JV knew another question was on its way. "And what about her humpback? Witcheth have humpbackth!"

JV sucked his teeth loudly. He was growing tired of the conversation. "Yeah, well, they also have warts on their noses, pointy hats, black cats, and ride around on brooms. Granny B is not a witch!"

JV swatted angrily at the leaves on either side as he ploughed through the forest. Carol, who had slowed to match her brother's pace, now trotted to keep up with JV's furious strides.

"You know, JV, I think we should probably stick to going in one direction," she said from somewhere behind him. "It'll make it a lot easier to find our way out again. Do you even know what direction we're heading in?"

JV made a quick guess. "I'd say northish."

"I don't think so," Carol said. "See how the tips of those high branches at the top are all pointing in one direction? Well, that's east. So we're actually heading northwest. And you know, you really should have thought to wear long sleeves and long pants like we did instead of that vest and shorts. Then you wouldn't get all scratched up and bitten."

When JV had first seen Carol and Pascal on the track, he had thought them crazy to be dressed as they were but had been too polite to point that out. *Too bad Carol couldn't return the favour*, he thought sourly. She was right, of course. It was a lot cooler here in the forest, and his exposed arms and legs already bore insect bites. But who really cared about stuff like that, anyway? They were there to explore.

"A few scratches and bites never killed anyone," he mumbled as he slapped at a mosquito on his shin. Behind him, Carol was saying something else.

"I think we should turn back, JV. It's probably around three thirty, and if Pascal and I get home late, Mummy won't let us come back to the forest with you again."

What could be better? JV thought wickedly. It was a fleeting thought, but he was still quite miffed that the excursion hadn't turned out as he had envisioned. He didn't feel as though they had gone far enough or seen anything of much interest as yet, just leaves, leaves, trees, trees, and more trees. He wasn't sure exactly what he had been expecting but knew there was something more to Oscuros that he needed to uncover.

"Let's just go a little farther. For another ten minutes or so." He didn't slow down and had gone a few more paces before realising that he no longer heard the snap of twigs or crunch of leaves behind him. *The least those two could do is try to keep up.* He turned around to tell Carol and Pascal just that and discovered that they were no longer following. There they stood, quite a way back, Carol with arms folded across her chest, looking peeved, and Pascal appearing torn between the urge to continue and not wanting to cross his sister.

"We're not going, JV," Carol said. "We have to head back. Now."

JV was in no mood to relent. Hoping to force another ten minutes out of them, he decided to change tactics.

"OK, well, since you're so good at directions, you'll have no problem getting back to the track without me."

For a moment, Carol's startled expression led JV to believe that he had won. Surely they would prefer to keep going with him for another measly ten minutes rather than find their way out alone. He said, "See ya," turned his back, and continued on. After a few paces, though, he wheeled around and was stunned to see no sign of Carol or Pascal. They had gone, disappeared. With a sinking feeling, he realised she had called his bluff and he regretted his behaviour.

He bit on the nail of his baby finger. He had a decision to make. Should he go after them or press on by himself? On one hand, they had come in together and should leave together. He was also at that place in the forest where the breadfruit tree stood like a sentinel over a greying boulder—the very spot that Granny B had cautioned him not to pass. Those were two very good reasons to call it a day. But on the other hand, Carol clearly had an excellent sense of direction and wouldn't have any trouble finding the track home. Plus, if he stayed in the forest, he could explore what lay beyond the breadfruit tree. His grandmother would never know.

※ ※ ※

As JV stepped past the boulder, he felt a surge of excitement tinged with apprehension. He was really doing it. He was heading into uncharted territory, and he was going it alone. Walking along, he couldn't help but enjoy his surroundings. There wasn't much difference in the landscape on this side of the boulder—there were still trees and leaves as far as the eye could see—but somehow his senses had sharpened. It seemed as though he was now aware of every sound, no matter how slight: from the rhythmic thud of his pulse to the gentle rustle of the leaves in the highest branches. He even heard the faint caw of a parrot and what sounded like the soothing gurgle of water somewhere in the distance.

His eyes were drawn upward to a flicker of movement in a nearby sandalwood tree. Was that a pair of eyes peeking out at him from the leaves? He kept very still. From behind the screen of foliage, small black leathery fingers inched tentatively along the thick branch. Now, two human-like hands and long arms covered in dark hair came into view. Finally, a white face slowly emerged, and JV, who had been holding his breath up to this point, exhaled with relief to find that he was looking into the big brown eyes of a capuchin monkey.

"Hey there, little fella. Came to keep me company?"

The monkey blinked, bent its head to one side as though considering JV's invitation, and then slowly moved forward to reveal its white chest and the rest of its body which ended in a rounded stub where his long, curling tail should have been.

"What happened to your tail?" JV asked.

The monkey looked back at his stump and then gazed down solemnly at JV.

"Don't want to talk about it, huh? Anything you want to share with me about the forest, then?" No response. "Well, I'm just going to keep heading this way, if you want to tag along."

JV started walking and kept up his one-sided conversation with the monkey who was following overhead, hopping along and adeptly jumping from tree to tree.

"You know," JV said as he tramped on, looking up at his hairy comrade, "if we're going to be friends, I'll have to come up with a name for you. It's only right. Let's see…Bob? No. Spunky? Nope." He cast a glance at the monkey's knobbed behind and shouted "I've got it. I'll call you Curty. Short for Curtail. Get it? I know you like—"

An earsplitting shriek from the monkey stopped JV in his tracks and then—thwack! Newly christened Curty had picked and hurled a hard green guava at JV, catching him squarely on the top of his head.

"Ouch!" JV yelled, rubbing the sore spot. "You're not a fan of the name, then? Well, if you can come up with something better, I'll change it, but until then I'm calling you Curty. And by the way, you're not the only one around here with good aim, you know. Bet I won't miss, even with you all the way up there."

He scanned the ground for the guava or some other useful projectile, and his eyes locked on what looked like a partially hidden, rusty lump of metal at his feet. He bent over to take a closer look and gulped. He had been inches away from stepping on a trap. If Curty hadn't screeched and thrown the guava… Then the truth hit him. Curty had known all about the trap and had saved him from getting caught in it. JV didn't have to guess how his little friend had lost his tail.

He had never seen a trap this close up before and shuddered to think of his own foot clamped between the two beastly rows of pointy iron teeth. It wasn't too difficult to imagine. He had seen such wounds on hunters who had somehow stumbled into their own traps and were brought to Granny B for healing. When they got to the house, they were never lucid enough to explain exactly how the accidents had occurred, and later on, when their faculties returned, they refused to talk of the incident. Some, like Arthur Samuel, gave up hunting altogether. JV stood and looked up at Curty.

"Thanks, buddy."

In acknowledgement, Curty jumped down to JV's shoulder and tugged on his ear. Reaching up, JV petted the silky fur.

"OK, well, let's keep going. Just give a tug if you see me getting too close to any other traps."

They continued on, JV telling Curty all about his life—school, friends, vacation plans, and Granny B—and Curty intently picking at JV's hair. Then, just as JV was relating the morning's happenings with Mr. Phipps, he stopped talking. With mouth agape, he slowly looked around in silent, wide-eyed wonder.

He was standing at the edge of a glade that could have been taken right out of a fairy tale. In the treeless clearing, golden beams of sunlight hit the earth which was covered in a downy layer of soft green moss; brown-and-white toadstools of varying sizes speckled the ground, and wild anthuriums and heliconias grew alongside a stream that opened into a dark pool framed with wet, slippery rocks. The scene was stunning, but it was the beautiful woman leaning out of the pond and stretched over one of the larger rocks who held JV's attention. Her chin rested on crossed arms, and her eyes were closed. Drops of water sparkled on her ebony shoulders like diamonds in the setting sun, and JV stood spellbound for what seemed like an eternity.

Then, without warning, her eyelids flicked up to reveal large greenish-gold orbs. She fixed them on JV, holding him in a stare that pierced to his very soul. He had the most curious sensation of detachment, as though he were no longer the master of his mind or body. Persistent tugs from Curty brought JV out of his trance, and in the split second that it took for JV to blink and refocus, the woman had disappeared.

"Did you see her, Curty? Where did she go?"

JV raced toward the pond, but there was no sign that anyone had been there: no footprints, not even a strand of hair left behind on the big rock. He peered over the boulder and into the water. The surface was smooth as glass, and only the faces of a baffled boy and a curious monkey looked out at him from the murky depths. He was sure he had not imagined her, but how could she have just vanished?

He stood for a moment looking at the reflection of the sinking sun on the water and remembered that he had to be out of the forest before dark. Although he wanted to stay to see if the woman would return, he knew better.

"I should get going," he said, glancing around the clearing one last time. "I really don't want to get caught out here with no light."

Moving swiftly, he retraced his steps to the track, all the while thinking of the mysterious woman at the pond. *What was her name? Where did she come from? Where did she go?*

He would just have to return to the glade tomorrow and wait for her. And perhaps Curty would show up again too. The strange little monkey had jumped off his shoulder close to where they had met earlier and bounded away without so much as a backward glance.

JV emerged from the forest as the last rays of sunlight vanished. He stepped onto the track toward home and then looked back at the trees. Was that children's laughter he heard or only the wind in the leaves? He thought of Carol and Pascal then and felt the early pricks of a guilty conscience. Surely they'd be safe at home by now. He dismissed the thought that they could still be in Oscuros and continued on his way. It was getting late.

Chapter 4

Stepping into the Dark

Urgent yells and a clamour of voices roused JV from sleep.

"What's going on?" he groaned. Through bleary eyes, he could see that it was still dark. He rolled over. The digital clock next to his bed showed 11:17 p.m. in bright red numbers.

He had returned home from the forest after seven o'clock that night to find Granny B on the front porch snoring lightly in her rocker. The second mug on the little wicker table, imprinted with a tell-tale orangey-crimson shade of lipstick, indicated that Doris's visit must have recently ended and that his poor grandmother was suffering the after effects of the ordeal. He had gently woken her, offered an arm for support, and helped her to bed. Thankfully she hadn't been alert enough to ask about his trip into Oscuros. She would have undoubtedly sussed out his less-than-stellar behaviour toward Carol and Pascal and somehow known that he had gone farther into the forest than he was allowed; both to his detriment.

By the time he had eaten supper, closed up the house for the night, and had a quick shower, it was eight o'clock—a little early to be turning in by vacation standards but a prudent choice. He wanted to be well rested to make proper amends to Carol and Pascal the next day and, of course, to try to find out more about the mystery lady by the pond.

But now he was being awoken from his sleep by the racket outside. So with heavy eyelids for the second time that day, he unwillingly got out of bed. He shuffled to the window, pulled the curtains back, peeped outside, and rubbed both eyes before peering again, this time squinting to get a better look.

Instead of the impenetrable darkness that usually stretched between his house and the forest, he saw flickering orange tongues from torches and pale-yellow spheres cast by lanterns. With eyes wide open now, he saw amidst the dancing cluster of lights a large group of villagers, their features distorted in an eerie glow, making enough noise to raise the dead. But from where he stood, he could neither identify any of the faces nor distinguish the words being yelled.

JV doubted Granny B would be awake, but he still shouted, "Heading out to see what's going on!" In less than two minutes, he was flying down the front porch steps, flashlight in one hand and slippers in the other. He tried to put them on as he ran toward the crowd that had positioned itself on the track before the forest. Nearing the group, he heard bits of conversation.

"She really missing? And what about the brother?"

"He not around…"

"…gone sometime earlier…"

"Need to check the forest…"

His head spun. With a mounting feeling of dread, he feared that the hubbub had to be about Carol and Pascal. They mustn't have made it out of the forest. A knot formed in his throat and his eyes welled with tears at the thought that because of his self-centredness, his two friends were now lost somewhere in Oscuros—probably hungry, tired, and very frightened. If only he had turned back when they had asked, all three of them would have made it out safely. There was no question about it—he had to go in and help find them.

He looked around and noted that most of the village was present. At the back of the assembly were the Simon boy and Patrick Chin with a cluster of other village youths. Up front and centre, impossible to miss in her multi-coloured hairnet, fuchsia nightgown, and matching robe, was Doris George of course, presumably trying to help but causing more confusion as far as he could tell. Even old Pa Gregory was there, standing off to the side.

JV inched closer to the front of the gathering, where Mr. Pearson was clearly in charge of the rescue effort. JV marvelled at him. How was he able to keep his composure with his children missing?

"Chin, Charles, Rollock, Ali, Jardine, and I will be leading groups into Oscuros," he shouted above the tumult. "If you're going in, it must be with one of us. Group leaders, know who's going in with you, and make sure you stick together. We're not losing anyone else tonight. And don't forget to watch out for traps."

JV was just thinking through what he was going to say to the father of his missing friends when Mr. Pearson caught sight of him, whispered a quick something to Mr. Charles at his side, and made his way through the crowd toward him.

Distraught, JV found it hard to look the approaching man directly in the eyes. What should he say? How should he begin? Before he could come up with an answer to either question, all six feet two inches of Mr. Pearson were towering over him, and he was wishing that he could somehow shrink into his slippers.

"Just the person I wanted to see," Mr. Pearson said, frowning. JV gulped, still unable to find his voice. "You went into Oscuros this afternoon with my children, didn't you?"

"Y-y-yes, sir," JV whispered, head bowed.

"And the three of you decided to leave separately?"

46

The tears that JV had been holding at bay began to run freely down his cheeks, and he looked up sorrowfully.

"It's all my fault!" he blurted out. "I should never have let them leave without me. It's just that I was so excited to go exploring and we hadn't seen anything interesting as yet, and Carol wanted to turn back so they wouldn't get home late, but I decided to continue on for a few more minutes, and now they're lost and wandering around somewhere in there." He gestured toward the black trees.

Mr. Pearson laid a hand on JV's shoulder. "Calm down, son," he said. "What's this about Carol and Pascal? They're at home as we speak, safe and sound. They were a little rattled when I caught them trying to sneak in the house, and they wouldn't tell me much about the trip, but they're OK." He paused and gave JV a meaningful look. "Of course, we had a serious chat about their getting home later than we had agreed on."

The reprimand barely registered with JV. His mind was processing the wonderful news that his friends were OK while simultaneously trying to figure out what was really going on. "Then who's missing?" he asked.

Mr. Pearson glanced at a small group that had broken off to the right of where they were standing. "Little Adelle De Couteau," he murmured. "No one can find her anywhere. And that's what I wanted to ask you. Did you see any sign of her in the forest or on your way home earlier?"

JV shook his head slowly. "No, I didn't see anyone else except for…"

47

"Who?" Mr. Pearson asked quickly, his eyebrows raised.

JV had been about to mention the lady at the pond but was beginning to have his doubts about her existence. The more he thought of her, the less likely the whole thing seemed. No one else could confirm what he saw, or thought he saw, and she had disappeared much too quickly. The encounter had also had an eerie, almost surreal quality to it, so his eyes could have been playing tricks on him. No, there wasn't any reason to say something that would make him look like a fool or a potential patient of St. Maurus—the island's mental hospital.

"I was only going to say Carol and Pascal," he finished.

"Oh." Mr. Pearson sighed. His eyes wandered again to the group at the fringe of the gathering.

JV followed his gaze and noticed that Earl De Couteau was at the centre of the small circle, his eyes more hollow and cheeks more sunken than usual. He was leaning heavily on another man, and those around him were expressing their solidarity with gentle pats on the back and light squeezes to his shoulders. JV didn't see Paulette De Couteau anywhere. He thought of how tired and disheartened she had seemed that morning at the market. JV pictured her waiting at home for her daughter, praying that Adelle would return to them.

"Well, all right, then," Mr. Pearson said, looking again at JV. "I'm going to get this search started. Let me know if you remember anything that could be useful." He walked away, and JV watched as the crowd slowly began to separate into groups.

Making his way to the nearest search party, JV realised that something was nagging at him. *What was it that Mason had said in the market when Mrs. De Couteau had complained about Adelle's previous disappearance? Something about baby animals?* JV tried to wrap his head around the memory and wondered whether it could be a clue to her whereabouts.

Standing at the back of a group of seven, he listened as Mr. Chin did a head count. The fishmonger looked at each face intently for a few seconds, then with his characteristic quick-fire delivery recapped all the dos and don'ts of the forest, asked if there were any questions, and said, "Good, let's get going." With lantern held high and a brisk pace, Mr. Chin led his group down the track toward the dark mouth of Oscuros.

✳ ✳ ✳

As they crossed into the untamed territory, JV immediately understood why Granny B always insisted that he make sure the trees were behind him before nightfall. The gloomy forest that let in very little light between its heavy boughs during the day turned into a sinister monster once the sun had set. The blackness was like a pack of hungry wolves, menacing the group with every step, clawing at their heels and forming a tight circle around them. Even the lanterns and flashlights that they brandished lost their potency and were almost completely absorbed by the darkness. This wooded world where silence seemed to reign during the daylight hours was replaced by a living, breathing entity that creaked, hissed, grunted, rustled, and hooted.

49

Being the youngest, JV had been ushered to the middle of the group, with Mr. Chin in front, two others on either side, and the Simon boy, Randall, bringing up the rear. JV was happy with the formation except for his lack of confidence in the scraggly teen's ability to provide any protection should they be attacked from behind.

"Growl!"

JV leapt into the air as a vicious snarl with its accompanying hot breath forced its way directly into his ear. Behind him, Randall howled with laughter.

"Nice jump, little man, nice jump! You should play basketball," he said, grinning and clapping. "Or not! You're way too short for that."

Mr. Chin, usually a good-tempered soul, whipped around and pointed at Randall. "Boy, you better stop your foolishness. We're not in here for fun, you know!"

"Yes, sir!" Still snickering, Randall gave Mr. Chin a mock salute.

They trudged along, calling Adelle's name and faintly hearing other voices do the same above the sounds of the forest. JV was so focused on detecting even the smallest sign of her presence that he didn't immediately notice how quiet Randall had become. When he did turn around to see what the mischief-maker was up to, he found that his rear guard was no longer there.

"These pranks have got to stop," JV said under his breath. Then he spied a shadowy figure dart behind the trees a few yards back to the left. He inhaled sharply and shone his flashlight at the spot. The only movement he saw, however, came from a bat crawling up the cracked bark of one of the trunks. He inched closer, squeezing the flashlight in both hands before him, imagining that its beam was also a shield against all the terrible creatures that could lunge for him at any moment.

"Cut it out, Randall!" he shouted. "This isn't funny."

There was no reply.

By this time, the group had stopped moving forward. Mr. Chin had doubled back and was now standing next to JV.

"What's going on?" Chin asked, the light from his lantern bobbing and weaving as he gesticulated. "Where's that silly boy?"

"Not sure," JV replied, "but I think he may be behind those trees back there." His flashlight was still aimed at the trunks, and Mr. Chin's eyes followed the beam.

"Randall, boy, you better pray I don't find you playing the fool behind there," Mr. Chin shouted, marching toward the trees. "If I were a different kind of man, I would leave you in this forest tonight. That would teach you a good lesson." But just as Mr. Chin neared the presumed hideout, Randall came sauntering out of the bushes from the opposite direction. JV, not expecting to see him emerge from the right, did a double take.

"Wait a minute...How did you get all the way over there?" he asked, flicking his light back and forth between the spot where he thought Randall had been hiding and where the young man, now unquestionably the object of everyone's vexation, was standing. But JV's question never received a reply. Randall had barely rejoined the group when Mr. Chin stalked across, closing the distance between them with swift strides, then grabbed him by the shoulders.

"You think this is a game?" he barked. "You like wasting people's time when a little girl may be lost out here in the dark? This is a joke to you?"

Randall shrugged free and took a step back, holding up his arms. "Hey, ease up, old man," he said. "I just needed a little privacy to take a leak, you know?"

Mr. Chin opened his mouth as if to say something and then shut it again. He glared at Randall until the boy looked away.

With everyone now gathered around, Mr. Chin cleared his throat, raised his lantern, and said the words JV had dreaded hearing: that it was time to call off the search and head back to the village. Mr. Chin pointed out that despite having spent hours in Oscuros, they had failed to find Adelle or anything that could lead them to her, and there was little more that they could do, as tired as they were.

Having made the decision to leave, the group reestablished its formation (this time with Randall up front with Mr. Chin) and began retracing its steps out of Oscuros. Despite his disappointment over the failed mission, JV remained on the lookout for Adelle, but also for tall, lurking shadows as well as the mystery woman's yellow-green eyes, which he assumed would glow in the dark. There was now, he noted with alarm, an ever-growing list of things linked to Oscuros that warranted further investigation.

The trip out of the forest seemed shorter than expected, but JV still released a sigh of relief once his back was to the final stand of trees and he could look up and see the twinkling stars in the night sky. His group was the last to emerge from Oscuros. The crowd before them was silent, mostly still, and full of sagging shoulders. The faces within it lit up momentarily as JV and the others approached, only to quickly lose any trace of optimism when they realised that Adelle was not among the new arrivals.

No one seemed to know what to do next. Mr. De Couteau, who had been too ill to venture into the forest, was led away sobbing. The villagers began to disperse. Within minutes, only a few persons were left behind talking in smaller groups, including Doris George and her two neighbours, who were rehashing the night's events.

"And that is why I doh let my children anywhere near that forest," Mr. Tolbert was saying. His arms were crossed tightly over his chest and his mouth was set in a hard line. The others nodded.

"Well, I'm still sure it's that Tricky Dixon criminal," Doris declared. "I know he took her. It was only this morning I was tellin' everybody that Alcavere is just the place that jailbird would want to come. A two-by-four little village where no one would think to look for him. And see? That's exactly what happened. That convict was here, and he took little Adelle. Who knows if we ever goin' to see that sweet child again." She pulled a large handkerchief from the top of her nightgown and dabbed at her eyes.

"Now wait a minute, Doris," Miss Jean piped in. "Don't go jumping to conclusions. We don't know if that's what really happened here."

"Then where is she? Where'd the child go?" Doris countered.

Miss Jean looked back at the dark trees. "Well, it is Oscuros we're talking about. She might just show up one of these days at the edge of the forest, like Miss B's boy."

They moved off, still speculating about what had become of Adelle De Couteau. JV was standing nearby and had heard every word.

Chapter 5

The Box of Secrets

All was quiet in Alcavere. The first rays of sunlight were climbing over the hills, and the mist, suspended above the ground and loosely wrapped around the trees, was beginning to dissipate. Ordinarily, there would have been signs of life in the village by this time: fishermen heading down to the shore or on the water casting their nets, farmers starting a long day's work out in the fields, a youngster cycling around delivering the daily newspaper. But today was different. Most of the villagers were still asleep, having spent the night and early morning hours searching for Adelle.

JV was awake, though. More than two hours after overhearing what Miss Jean had said, there he was still sitting alone and puzzled on the front porch of the house, her cryptic words echoing in his head:

"She might just show up one of these days at the edge of the forest, like Miss B's boy."

What on earth had she been talking about? Miss B—Granny B—was his flesh and blood, and he had lived with her all of his life. True, his personal story was a little less straightforward than other children's, but the suggestion that he had been abandoned on the fringes of Oscuros was ridiculous. It was certainly no secret that he had been left in his grandmother's care when he was born and that his parents had died before they could return for him.

JV thought back to the very first time he had asked Granny B about them. He was five years old, had just started kindergarten, and had come home full of questions after a week of seeing young mothers and fathers collect his classmates at the end of each day. Where were his parents? Who were they? Why didn't he live with them? Confronted with the sudden interrogation, Granny B had pulled him up into her chair and wrapped both arms around him. He had snuggled against her chest, inhaling the scent of the herbal potpourri that always accompanied her. Then she had launched into the first of many tales of her daughter and son-in-law, two restless souls whose love of excitement and adventure had drawn them out of Alcavere and, within a month, their native land.

Propelled by a force comprehensible only to them, they had travelled north, up the archipelago of islands, and then traced the shores of the Caribbean Sea southward through Central and South America. Their letters were filled with news of the wonderful things they had seen and reminders to Granny B to give JV two kisses on their behalf and to make sure he knew how much he was loved.

These narratives became JV's favourite bedtime stories. As Granny B read, he was transported to extraordinary places: ruined pyramids of ancient civilisations, volcanic peaks, coral reefs, lush rain forests, and even a deep lake of liquid asphalt that, according to legend, had swallowed an entire Amerindian village. Although it had been a long time since Granny B had brought out the letters, he remembered each one in vivid detail. Those letters had made it possible for him to tag along on his parents' travels, albeit vicariously, and were, in essence, his only link to the two wanderers whose lives were cut short by a violent hurricane. His parents' written messages had become his anchor...his roots, and undoubtedly, the catalyst for his own hunger for adventure. And what's more, he realised they were just what he needed at that moment.

With thoughts of losing himself in pages of dramatic accounts overshadowing all other concerns, JV rose, shook the pins and needles from his legs, and entered the house. Granny B would be up by now.

Not surprisingly, he found her in the herb room. She always said she did her best thinking there. JV wondered how long she had been tucked away in her retreat—humming, pondering, and keeping busy. Peering in, he saw that her back was to the half-opened door and that she was grating a large avocado seed at the wooden counter that stretched from one end of the room to the other. The rest of the fruit lay exposed, its firm yellow-green flesh facing upward like empty sockets now that the seeds were removed. Numerous glass jars sat on the shelves lining the walls, each neatly labelled and containing some part of a plant or tree that would inevitably find its way into one of Granny B's healing rubs, balms, oils, or teas. In sharp contrast to the kitchen, this room was always kept meticulously clean and well-ordered, with everything put and kept in its rightful place, even the twef that JV had picked the previous day.

"Morning, Jason," Granny B said without turning around. "I heard there was a search for Adelle."

From Doris, no doubt, JV thought. He slid through the door and eased his way into the narrow room.

"How you could leave and not tell me anything?" Granny B continued. "You know how long I was up wondering about you?"

"Oh gosh, sorry, Granny," JV said, hoping that he wouldn't be in too much trouble. "It was late and I didn't want to wake you up."

She turned to him with hand on hip and eyebrow up. "Eh heh? Well, make sure you wake me up next time, you hear?"

"Yes, Granny."

She turned back to the avocado seed. "So no sign of Adelle, eh?"

"No, Granny. No luck. She's still missing."

"Well, I hope they find that child soon," she said, grating steadily. "Although…something's not sitting too well with me about this whole affair. Something's just not right. First she's sneaking out, then she's in punishment, and now she's gone? Eh, eh. There's more in the mortar than the pestle, if you ask me. Mark my words, Jason, I have a feeling in my bones that there's something somebody's not saying."

JV remembered that he had had a similar feeling. And like his grandmother, he was bothered that he still couldn't put the pieces together.

"Anyhow," Granny B continued, "hopefully someone will soon share whatever information they may have. But in the meantime, I'm sure Paulette and Earl aren't giving up on finding her. They'll also be trying to get word to Mason if they haven't managed to already."

The mention of Adelle's parents reminded JV of the purpose of his visit to the herb room.

"Granny?" he asked quietly.

"Yes, Jason?"

"Can I see the letters?"

She stopped her grating for a split second and then resumed. "The letters? I haven't pulled those out in years. And don't you have them all memorised from start to finish anyway?" she said.

"Yes, but I've never actually read them for myself before. I was too young."

She turned around and looked at JV. "Well, they're packed away up on the shelf in my cupboard, and I'm not sure how easy it will be to dig them out. You really need them now?"

"Please, Granny."

Granny B sighed, put down the grater and shuffled from the room. JV could hear her muttering to herself all the way down the corridor, then the thud of a stool being placed before the wardrobe, a groan as she stepped up onto it, followed by what sounded like packages being pushed and pulled.

A few minutes passed. JV was getting restless. *Can't she find them? Should I go and have a look myself?* It was a quick thought, but he knew better than to entertain it. There were two places in the house that were off-limits to him: the herb room, under normal circumstances, was one, and Granny B's cupboard, under all circumstances, was the other. But it still took an impressive amount of willpower to stay put and he was on the verge of calling out when Granny B came through the door with a large shoe box in hand. She rested it gently on the counter and went back to her grating without a word.

JV stepped closer and lifted the lid off the old box. Inside, lying across the rest of the contents was a detailed map of the Caribbean and the Americas. He looked at it briefly and put it aside, by doing so revealing two stacks of papers that were hidden underneath: one of magazine and newspaper clippings, and the other of loose white pages. Curious, he reached for the clippings first.

As he flipped through, a number of items grabbed his attention: articles on the Soufrière Hills eruptions in Montserrat, a lost group of hikers in Puerto Rico's El Yunque rain forest, Harrison's Cave in Barbados, the Diamond waterfall and mineral baths of St. Lucia, a Hindu temple in the sea in Trinidad, and many others. JV smiled proudly to think that although he had never once left his little village, all these places were familiar to him thanks to his parents. As with the map, he put the clippings aside and then turned his attention to the last thing left in the box: the stack of white pages. The letters.

Filled with anticipation, he reverently picked up the top page and turned it over so that he was looking at lines upon lines of blue writing. Yes, this was what he needed to put things back in perspective. To reclaim his inner sense of harmony and balance. To remind him that no matter what obstacles and difficulties he faced or insecurities he had, there was a whole wide world out there filled with places, people, and things that he would someday see with his own eyes.

He looked at the elegant cursive that filled the page, slanting to the right, and thought of how reassuring and yet curious it was that the penmanship should be so familiar. And then, in the instant that it took to glance up at the labels on the jars and back down again to the letter, a terrible notion began to scratch at his subconscious until it had skilfully and savagely clawed through to his conscious thought.

Unwilling as JV was to consider the intruding suspicion, he checked out the jar labels again. To his alarm, looped l's, h's, and f's as well as ornate capital i's and e's found their counterparts on the trembling page in his hands. He flipped through the sheets with increasing urgency. His heart raced as he saw that the handwriting on every last one was identical to that on the labels. It couldn't be true, but the proof was literally in his hands.

JV's head reeled. There were no adventures in other lands and no messages from his parents assuring him of their love: no proof that he was the person he had always thought himself to be; probably nothing to tie his blood to this woman who had once again stopped grating and was standing next to him, her face a canvas of remorse, fear, sorrow, and pity; and no evidence to say that he was anything other than an orphan who had been abandoned on the fringe of the forest.

As the full weight of all these realizations hit him, JV's hands went cold, and the pages slipped from his fingers. Unable to fully process the sudden onslaught of shock, grief, and anger, he was barely able to register Granny B's touch steadily guiding him to the only chair in the room. Once seated, all he could do was stare blankly at the pages that he had regarded mere seconds before as a sort of lifeline, now scattered across the floor. So many emotions, questions, and accusations. Such a profound need to cry, yell, and then cry some more. The first three words that made it out of his mouth were profound in their simplicity.

"Who am I?" he whispered.

Not meeting his gaze, Granny B bent down and started retrieving the pages. When she straightened up, she looked him directly in the eyes.

"Who are you?" she repeated. Her voice was steady, her tone firm. "You are Jason Felix Theodore Valentine. A twelve-year-old Form Two student who does well in school, whose favourite subjects are geography and English, who has a healthy appetite, an even healthier sense of curiosity, and good, solid friends.

"You were the baby who skipped crawling and went straight to walking, who said his first real word before he had a single tooth in his mouth. The boy who can probably name every plant on this island and knows something about most of the countries in our part of the world. You are the same person who made a special Christmas card last year for lonely old Pa Gregory and who just spent the whole night and early morning hours looking for a little girl who may be lost in the forest."

Granny B had built up steam and her eyes were flashing.

"You are Jason Felix Theodore Valentine. You can question your origins and the identity of your parents—you have a right to and you should—but don't you ever question who you are!"

Fat tears finally began to roll down JV's cheeks. He could barely find his voice.

"So it's true, then. What Miss Jean said about me? That I was found at the edge of the forest?"

Granny B rested the jumble of pages on the counter, turned to face JV once again, and leaned back. She took a deep breath and began.

"It was November the second. All Souls'. The darkness that wraps itself around Alcavere at night, almost swallowing our tiny village whole, was driven away that evening. Every doorstep and wall was lit with candles, each one to remind us of someone we had lost. And the cemetery...oh, the cemetery was like a shining city, ablaze with flambeaux and countless candles on gravestones, columns, and shrines. They were even on the paths between the graves, standing like lines of sentinels of various heights and colours. And the air was heavy with the scent of all those flowers—hibiscuses, orchids, roses, ginger lilies—bunches of them adorning the final resting place of so many of my neighbours and friends.

"It was getting late, and only a few of us were still there at the graveyard despite the hour on a night like that when duppies, jumbies, and other spirits are roaming free. Yes...I remember it as if it was just yesterday: Miss Jean, not too far away, bowing over her husband's headstone, her fingers working the rosary beads; Harry and Vera Tolbert, who had just buried their first born the day before, standing as still as statues in front the little grave where the earth was still loose and fresh; and a small group making its exit under the wrought-iron arches. Everything quiet, quiet.

"Then I heard it. Carried on the night breeze that was tugging at the flames, I heard the faintest wail, like the meow of a kitten. Scanning the cemetery, the only movement I saw was the flickering shadows cast by the candlelight. Tired and ready to leave, I was about to pass under the arches myself when I heard it again but this time louder, more insistent. Definitely not the cry of a kitten.

"I looked back at Miss Jean and knew that she had heard it too. She was standing, clutching the rosary in both hands, her eyes wide. The Tolberts had also heard the sound and were craning their necks this way and that trying to figure out where it had come from. Of the four of us, Miss Jean was the first to say something. 'The duppies are out tonight. You hear them?' And as if right on cue, we heard another long, plaintive cry. 'But that sounds like a child…a baby,' Vera said. She grabbed hold of her husband and stared down at the grave before them, perhaps thinking of what she would have given to hear her own daughter's voice again. Then Miss Jean stepped closer. 'You don't see? That's just what those evil spirits want you to think,' she explained. 'That it's some little child you're hearing, so that you go out looking and—BAM!—they grab you and carry you off.'

"But Harry wasn't having any of it. He sucked his teeth and said, 'That is a set of nonsense, Jean, and you know it. Don't be scaring Vera like that. That ain't no duppy, child, or duppy pretending to be a child. Just an animal out there in the forest. I don't know about the two of you, but we're heading home.'

"Harry and Vera started walking past me on their way out of the cemetery with Miss Jean close behind, and they had almost cleared the arches when I called after them, 'But what if it really is a child? We can't leave a child out here.' But they didn't pay me any mind. 'Go home, Miss B,' Harry shouted back. And then Miss Jean yelled, 'I hope you remembered to put rice round your house so the duppies don't follow you inside.' I could still hear her going on about the spirits, her voice fading as they got farther away. Then, just like that, I was alone."

Granny B paused, her eyes staring off into the distance. JV sat as still as stone, barely breathing.

"So what happened next?" he managed to ask.

"Well, duppy or not, I had to check things out. I listened again for the cry and left the graveyard through the side gate, facing the forest. There wasn't a star in the sky, and the night was so dark that even with all the light from the cemetery and village, I could just barely make my way along the path to Oscuros. I went slowly, stopping each time I heard the sound to make sure I was heading in the right direction. Walk, stop, walk, stop…until I was too tired to take another step. So I sat where I was and gave my old legs a rest.

"The minutes passed, and I listened for the cry but only heard the steady chirp of invisible frogs and crickets, their songs interrupted by occasional squeaks from bats flying overhead. I still wasn't sure of what I was going to find or, truth be told, what would find me. It wasn't until a jumbie bird hooted, its ominous call predicting the death of someone nearby that I definitely knew I was following the cries of an infant, not a cunning spirit, and that I needed to get to the child soon. But where was it? Panicking, I said the fastest and most important prayer of my life: 'One more sound, little one...just one more, and I will find you. Don't give up on me yet.'"

Granny B looked tenderly at JV. He was sitting with his feet up on the chair, arms around his legs, and chin resting on his knees. She went on.

"No sooner had the last word passed my lips than I heard a short whimper coming from somewhere just ahead. I started walking again but this time with a fresh sense of purpose. Oscuros loomed before me, and although I had made up my mind to enter if necessary, I really hoped that I wouldn't have to do the unthinkable and go in a forest on All Souls' night. Then, just mere feet from the first stand of trees, something on the ground by the bush to the side caught my eye. I went across. It was a triangle of white cloth, hanging over the edge of a basket. I peered in the basket and saw that the rest of the cloth was swaddled around a little body, leaving only a round brown face exposed...your sweet, angelic face, Jason. But your eyes were closed, and you were deathly still. Fearing that I was too late, I picked you up, put my finger under your nose, and hoped for a sign of life. I have never known such relief as when I felt those steady wisps of warm air. I stood there for a few minutes, holding you close, then put you back in your basket and brought you home."

Granny B sighed, shaking her head slowly.

"Believe me, Jason, despite my best efforts, I never learned where you came from or how you ended up at the forest. All I know is that we didn't give up on each other that night and that I have loved you as my very own ever since."

Silence reigned as Granny B's words hung in the air. JV hid his face behind his knees, and the only movement he made was to raise an arm to wipe away a tear. The minutes ticked by. When he finally spoke, he did so in a muffled voice.

"And the letters? You made up all those stories, wrote them down, and pretended they were from my parents? Why did you lie? Why didn't you just tell me the truth?"

"I'm sorry, Jason," she replied wearily. "Perhaps I was wrong. But how do you tell a five-year-old that he had been abandoned? How do you explain to him that even though one life had left him behind, it wasn't the end of the world because another had embraced him with open arms? That he had become the single most important person to an old woman who had never had children of her own but who knew from the moment she first held him in her arms and felt his heart against hers that he was where he should be...that he was home?" she asked. "I knew I would have to explain things to you someday, but when you came home with all those questions, they caught me off guard. I thought I had more time than I did, and I wasn't prepared. So instead of telling you the truth, I created a story. One that took a five-year-old's mind off of his parents' absence and created an outlet for his brilliant imagination; one that made him look out and not in; one that prodded him to eagerly await the possibilities of the future rather than brood over the misfortunes of the past."

JV thought of all the nights he had listened to those stories that had shaped his childhood, and remembered lying in bed imagining himself as an explorer, longing for the day when he could retrace his parents' footsteps throughout the Caribbean. But now that he knew the truth, his happiest memories seemed absurd, and he couldn't help feeling as though he had lost everything, even his dreams. How could things have changed so abruptly and how could Granny B (if he could even call her that anymore) expect him to feel like the same person?

Suddenly, he was exhausted. The recent revelations, together with his lack of sleep, had taken their toll, and at that moment, there was nothing more he could think to ask, nothing else he wanted to know. He got up slowly from the chair and looked past the grey, hunched old lady as he headed to the door. She was saying something else as he left: something about love, the true meaning of family, and unbreakable bonds. But he was too tired to listen, too sad to care. Maybe, just maybe, if he lay down and closed his eyes, this bad dream would be over, and he could be JV once again—JV the explorer, JV the adventurer.

Chapter 6

Making Amends

The first beads of rain came tentatively, escaping the swollen, charcoal-grey clouds and falling down, down, down until finally hitting the thirsty soil where they were devoured so quickly that their fleeting existence went mostly unnoticed. But the villagers, whose gazes had been upturned for more than a month waiting for the prolonged dry spell to come to an end and the skies to burst open, could not miss the fatter, more confident drops that followed—pinging on their galvanised roofs like crisp, dulcet notes from a thousand steel pans.

Eager faces appeared at windows, peering out as the plump drops became long, wet cords seemingly connecting the heavens to the earth, and in no time at all, the children of Alcavere were streaming outside to splash in the newly formed puddles.

The rainy season had arrived at last.

But by the end of the second straight day of continuous showers, the joy of receiving such abundant rainfall had begun to fade. Villagers watched uneasily as roadside gutters overflowed and water crept ever closer to their front steps. They shook their heads in dismay when they glanced over at the scorched hillsides that had not only endured seven months of unrelenting heat but had also suffered further abuse because of indiscriminate burning. Knowing it was too late to reverse the damage, the people of Alcavere could only hope that the loose soil did not slip down the slopes and bury them all under thick layers of dense mud.

Apart from the threat of flooding, another unfortunate effect of the rain was that any clues relating to Adelle's whereabouts that may have been missed were forever washed away, making the odds of finding her steeper yet. But even so, no effort that could lead to her return was spared in those first seventy-two hours.

Uniformed detectives had come from Landing Town, taken statements, conducted a thorough inspection of the village, and left. Flyers bearing a picture of a smiling girl with two shoulder-length braids found their way to neighbouring towns, and a few stout souls had even tried to search Oscuros again, only to give up, disheartened, soon afterward.

What else could be done? No one dared say it openly, but JV knew that the villagers were losing any hope of finding the little girl with the bright eyes and ready smile.

And Adelle's parents? Having exhausted all conceivable avenues in the quest to find their daughter and at a loss as to what more they could possibly do, Paulette and Earl De Couteau remained at home, receiving solemn-faced visitors and marking time until Mason's return. JV wondered at Mason's continued absence, but the rumour swirling through the village, which had reached JV's ears during one of Doris's visits with Granny B, was that Mason had been in touch and was still in Landing Town, trapped in a part of the capital that was inundated by flood waters. His promise to return to Alcavere as soon as he could was apparently his parents' last ray of hope. They told everyone who stopped by that Mason would not rest until his sister was found.

※ ※ ※

The following day brought no new word on Adelle but was accompanied by two positive developments. The first was that, to everyone's relief, the weather at last seemed to settle into the familiar rainy-season pattern of bright, blue sunny mornings that only lapsed into a downpour around mid-afternoon. The second was that JV, who had been ensconced in his room and had barely spoken a word to Granny B since she had told him the truth about his past, had finally decided to emerge from his self-imposed seclusion. The pull of the forest had intensified, plus, he had done a lot of thinking over the past three days. Though the reality of his origins still stung, he recognised that there was a lot for which he had to be grateful.

What would have happened, for instance, if Granny B hadn't found him on that All Souls' night and adopted him as her own? How much longer would he have lasted out there before succumbing to the elements or becoming a tasty morsel for one of the wild animals that prowled the forest? Reflecting on his life thus far, he saw that he had been well loved and taken care of and had wanted for nothing. It was time to stop moping.

JV opened his bedroom door and stepped out into the corridor. Expecting to find Granny B sipping tea at the table, he went to the kitchen but only saw Kockot taking a mid-morning nap at her perch, standing on one leg with her head turned backward and her beak nestled under a wing. He approached the window and peered through. The plants looked rejuvenated, and glistening water droplets made him think of a world that had been washed sparkling clean of many months' worth of dust. Everything seemed to shine, everything, that is, except for Granny B's car, which was still parked in its usual spot and plastered with mud-splattered leaves from the soursop tree. He was thinking of just how much work would be needed to get all that stuff off when a slow, rhythmic creaking caught his attention.

Stepping outside, he was immediately hit by the heavy smell of wet earth. It wasn't an unpleasant odour but a little overwhelming for a nose that had been shut up indoors for days.

"Amazing, isn't it?" Granny B asked from her rocker. "Too little rain, then too much. Even Mother Nature has a hard time getting things right sometimes."

JV knew Granny B too well not to understand the hidden meaning behind her words. Although her apology was indirect, it had the same effect on him as if she had jumped up in mid-rock, clasped her hands together, and begged for his forgiveness.

"Well, she is only human, after all," he responded. Recognising that all was forgiven between them, they shared a smile. "Do you know that I was this close to running away the other day?" he mentioned a few moments later, holding up his thumb and index finger and showing Granny B the small space between the two.

"What? In all that rain?"

"Yeah, well, I didn't really think about that part. I thought that I could go looking for my parents. Or at least try to find out more about them...somehow."

"Where were you going to start?"

JV shrugged.

"So what happened? Why did you change your mind?"

"Well, I figured I'd stick around a little while longer since you're not getting any younger and need some looking after."

"Well, that's real nice of you, Jason, and I sure appreciate it," Granny B said. JV could see she was trying her best to stifle a laugh. "I've certainly raised a true gentleman, haven't I?" She patted his hand, then looked up at the sky. "Nice and bright today, eh? Some real good sunshine out here. Would be a shame to waste this nice morning sun." She glanced at the car.

"Yep. I've got lots to do before the rain starts up again, Granny. Like go check on Carol and Pascal. I haven't had a chance to see them since we went exploring and…well…" Remembering his bad behaviour toward his friends, he bowed his head and studied the ground.

"And you have something important you need to tell them, don't you?" Granny B concluded.

"Yes. Plus, I'm not done exploring Oscuros. I thought about what you said, and there's still a lot I want to see and discover, but instead of following in my imaginary parents' footsteps, I'll just make my own." He paused and caught Granny B stealing another glance at the car.

"Mmm-hmm. Once those footsteps don't go past the breadfruit tree," she said, watching him carefully. JV felt his chest tighten.

"Yeah, lots to do, so I better get started, especially since it's going to take me a while to get that to look anything close to how it should." He pointed at the muddy mess under the soursop tree and scampered off to find a bucket and hose.

❋ ❋ ❋

Almost three hours later, JV was on his way to Carol and Pascal's house. He was in a good mood. He had not only made up with Granny B but also had a bellyful of crab and callaloo, rice, and fried plantains—all washed down with a tall glass of cold mauby. Cleaning the old Cortina had been exercise enough, but after a meal like that, he really needed the walk. The weather was holding up nicely, and once he had apologised to Carol and Pascal and was back on their good side, he planned to take them to the clearing in the forest where he'd seen the mysterious lady.

As he neared his destination, he saw Mrs. Pearson outside sweeping her garden path. He approached the gate, but when she looked up and pressed her mouth into a hard line on seeing him, he knew he wasn't exactly in her good books. She stopped her sweeping, held on to the broom with one hand, and placed the other on her hip.

"Good afternoon, Miss Sandra," he said.

"Jason."

"Um, are Carol and Pascal at home?"

One of her eyebrows shot up, and her face creased into a scowl. "I don't think…" she began, but then a cheery voice called out from the large bay window overlooking the yard.

"Hiya, JV!" Pascal shouted, waving enthusiastically.

Failing to hide her exasperation, Mrs. Pearson took a deep breath and instructed JV to wait where he was, which he did while he watched her march up the path to the front porch steps and then into the house. Pascal's face disappeared from the window moments later.

In the minutes that followed, JV prepared his apology, deciding that short and sweet would be the best way to go. Humbling himself before Carol would be painful enough without having it drag on and on. He had rehearsed what he was going to say at least three times and was just beginning to think that perhaps Mrs. Pearson wasn't going to let them come out to him when the door opened and Carol appeared with a considerably less exuberant Pascal in tow.

"What's up, JV?" she asked dryly as she approached the gate. "You know, if you keep biting your nails like that, you won't have any left."

JV hastily clasped his hands behind his back. "Um...I just wanted to pass by and tell you and Pascal that I shouldn't have left you alone to find your way out of the forest the other day. I'm really sorry. I hope it wasn't too difficult to get out."

Pascal's head jerked up and he opened his mouth as if to say something, but before he could get a word out, Carol grabbed his arm and jumped in.

"You should be sorry, JV. That was not cool. Not cool at all. We actually did run into some trouble, you know."

"Yeah, we—"

"But we found our way out in the end, though, didn't we?" she snapped at Pascal, giving him a sharp look.

"Well, I'm just glad you got home all right," JV added.

Carol relaxed a bit and appeared to consider things for a couple seconds. "Apology accepted," she finally yielded. "Just don't let it ever happen again."

"Friends?" JV asked, extending his hand.

"Yeah...friends." She smiled, thrusting her free one out and giving JV a firm shake.

Now that the unpleasant part was taken care of, JV had other matters to discuss. He looked her in the eyes.

"I've been thinking it over, and there's something else that I've decided I should tell you," he said, lowering his voice. Carol leaned in just the slightest bit.

"Yes?" she responded, her eyes widening.

"Well, you're not going to believe this…I mean, I hardly believe it myself, but—"

"But what, JV?" The faintest of smiles was beginning to tug at the corners of her mouth.

"Well," he continued, "the strangest thing happened after you guys left Oscuros. I saw this woman…or girl…I'm not really too sure because I couldn't see her that well, but—"

"Huh?" Carol interrupted, her face falling. "What woman? What girl?" She took a step back.

"Well…um…" JV hesitated, momentarily thrown off by his friend's reaction.

Pascal, no longer able to contain himself and taking advantage of his sister's discomposure and JV's bewilderment, blurted out, "We thaw her too! Her and her friendth. They had thtraw hatth, and their FEET!" But poor Pascal. That was about all he managed to say before Carol re-collected herself and shushed him up.

Thoroughly confused, JV was about to ask a few questions of his own when Mrs. Pearson, who had been keeping a close eye on things under the guise of sweeping the steps and porch, signalled that it was time for Carol and Pascal to return indoors. Clearly she thought that the visit had gone on long enough.

"Wait!" JV said before they turned to leave. From the looks of things, it didn't seem like he'd be able to take them to the clearing that day, but at least they could make plans for the next morning. "Want to take another trip in with me tomorrow if there's no rain?" he asked, imagining their faces when they saw the glade.

"Are you kidding?" Carol shot back. There was disbelief in her eyes but also a hefty dose of fear. "We're not going anywhere near Oscuros. There's no way our parents would let us go. For one thing, they were really angry when we got home late last time—we're actually still grounded because of it—and for another, Mummy hasn't let us out of her sight since Adelle disappeared." She nodded toward the house where Mrs. Pearson had given up the broom as a prop and was now standing with both hands on her hips and glowering down at them. "There's just no way. Sorry." Carol turned away from JV, unwilling to test the limits of her mother's patience any longer. "And if you know what's good for you, you'll stay away from Oscuros too."

"Yeah. Watch out for the—"

"Oh, hush, Pascal!" she said. With that, the visit was brought to an end, and JV watched in disappointment as Carol ushered her brother up the path before her.

Chapter 7

A Hidden Horror

Perhaps JV should have been a bit more receptive to Carol's advice and not been so quick to dismiss her warnings, but the truth was that he just couldn't stay away from Oscuros. He had told Granny B earlier that he wanted to continue exploring the forest—which was accurate enough since there was definitely something drawing him there—but a certain mysterious lady had also been lodged firmly in his mind ever since his last visit. He had been thinking of her frequently, although whenever he recalled the moment that her eyes flashed open, he would be thrust from the memory and catapulted back into the here and now.

JV was determined not to share his experience in the glade with anyone else. It was only after much internal back-and-forth that he had eventually decided to let Carol and Pascal in on his secret, partly as a peace offering and partly because he found it increasingly difficult to keep what he had seen to himself. But even after putting so much thought into the decision, he hadn't had a chance to tell them anything of substance. Carol had totally freaked him out with her odd reaction to his first few words, and at the time, Pascal's outburst about hats and feet had only added to his confusion. JV was beginning to consider that the beings that he and his friends had separately encountered in Oscuros that day were somehow connected, although he also realised that he couldn't be sure without more information. The question was where to start since Carol had made it clear he wasn't going to get much else out of them.

JV contemplated all of this as he wound his way through Oscuros. It also occurred to him that the person who had abandoned him may have passed the same way twelve years before. He kept an eye out for Curty and hoped that his vague memory of how he had found the clearing would prove sufficient to locate it again. He hadn't seen any distinctive landmarks since passing the breadfruit tree, although a general feeling of familiarity did provide some measure of reassurance that he was going in the right direction. A few more steps and he was finally satisfied he was close. This was the spot where the heliconias grew closer together and...yes, here was the low-lying branch wrapped tightly with woody vines that he had almost hit his head on the last time and which he was now careful to duck beneath.

JV's excitement at knowing that he was on the right track turned to elation some paces later when, on making a final push through the trees, he found himself awed once again by the captivating beauty of the glade. He had done it. He had reached his sanctuary in the forest and was on the verge of stepping completely out into the open, when he remembered his sole purpose for being there: to see the lady once more. She had disappeared so quickly upon noticing him the last time that perhaps it would be a good idea to keep himself hidden, at least initially. He stepped back into the foliage and crouched down to wait. His vantage point offered an unrestricted view of the pond, and the only thing left to hope for was that the mystery lady would in fact make an appearance.

JV's legs cramped as the time dragged on. The incessant buzz of mosquitoes around his ears began to work on the last scraps of his patience, and he started to recognize that his plan may not have been all that great. There was no reason to believe that she would be there at that particular time and on that very day, or would even return to the pond at all. He had neither seen her before nor since the encounter. For all he knew, she could have just been a traveller passing through. Honestly, what were the odds that he would ever see her again?

JV was reflecting on how nice it would have been if all of this had dawned on him before, when he heard voices. He squatted even lower and listened. Nothing. An agonising minute passed. Then from the corner of his eye, he detected a stir of movement between the trees on the other side of the clearing. His stomach did a quick lurch out of excitement, anticipation, and fear. His breathing became shallow. He was on high alert. Surely the thumping of his pulse couldn't actually be as deafeningly loud as he perceived it to be.

Keeping very still and hoping that he was adequately hidden, he looked on as a tall, well-built man broke free of the vegetation and walked into the clearing. He was wearing camouflage pants and gripping a cutlass, its broad blade almost long enough to brush the heel of his rugged black boots. His other hand held the neck of a sack that was slung over his shoulder. There was more rustling of leaves and then a second man, shorter and stockier than the first, came into view. He too was dressed in camouflage and toted a large bag but, instead of a cutlass, he was armed with a rifle.

JV's first reaction on seeing the intruders was annoyance. Their presence would probably ruin any chance he had, however slim, of his mystery lady showing herself. But sensing the potential for intrigue, JV decided to stay where he was and observe. Once the second man had made it fully into the clearing, both men went directly to the large rock, where they dropped their sacks and weapons.

"I'm telling you, that was the biggest snake I ever saw," the short, stocky guy said to his partner as he pulled off his boots. He had a nasal, almost whiny voice. "I didn't even see all of it, it was so long, but its width…man, it was thick like…like…like that stump over there," he said, pointing at a two-foot wide log lying a few feet in front of JV's hiding place. JV put down his head and tried to make himself as small as possible.

Mr. Cutlass, as JV had named the first man in his mind, laughed and sucked his teeth. "You keep talking about this megasnake. Plenty, plenty talk. But how come you're the only one who ever saw it? Eh?" He had stripped down to his shorts and waded toward the centre of the pond. His back was criss-crossed with old scars, but there was a fresh wound—an angry-looking scratch along the side of his neck—that he began to wash gingerly.

"Man, I was lucky to see it," Stocky continued, easing into the water. "That thing moved so fast. I saw piece of it one minute, and then—zip!—it was gone. But I'm telling you, if I find that snake, I'll be set for life. No more of this kinda work for me."

"Yeah, well, just make sure I'm there when you see it next time, 'cause I'll really have to see to believe."

"No prob, brother man. And if I'm in a good mood, I'll even let you help me catch it," Stocky said.

Cutlass disappeared under the water's surface for a few seconds before popping back up closer to the pond's edge and climbing out of the water.

"It's a good thing you noticed this place," Stocky continued, scrubbing under his arms and behind his ears. "I'm a fella who needs to bathe at least every three days or so. We may be stuck out here, but we're not animals." He let out a series of snorts and chuckles, strange sounds that were right at home in the forest.

Ignoring his partner's attempt at humour, Cutlass redid the last of the buttons on his shirt and then reached for his blade and sack. "Let's move," he said. "We should get back before you-know-who blows a fuse."

"Yeah, you're right," Stocky agreed, sloshing up the embankment. "That man gets crazy when he's angry. But he really needs to chill out, eh. Everything's going according to plan. By this time tomorrow, we're on easy street." He reached for his things on the rock. "So what you think of the new guy?" He started putting on his clothes and shoes.

Cutlass gave a quick shrug. "Not sure. Maybe a little too jumpy, but he has some serious talent with the hardware. I'll give him that."

"True, true." Stocky nodded. "Not the chattiest of fellas, though. But that's OK; I don't like people who talk all the time, anyhow." He slung the sack into its former position, picked up his rifle, and followed Cutlass toward the same spot in the trees where they had entered about fifteen minutes before, all the while maintaining his one-sided conversation.

By this time, JV was beside himself with curiosity. Who were they? Where were they going, and what was in those sacks? He watched as the back of Stocky's head disappeared from view and then got to his feet slowly. There had been no sign of the lady he had come to see but JV had stumbled onto something else that required investigation. He would need to be careful not to be seen or heard.

❋ ❋ ❋

JV found the task of tailing the two men to be more complicated than he had anticipated. He proceeded as quietly as he could, making sure to stop whenever they came to a halt. He had to be painstakingly cautious. But he was also trying to keep track of the turns they were making—north, east, northeast, and east again—hoping that he would remember it all when it was time for him to leave.

"Shh! Listen. You hear that?" Cutlass's hoarse whisper pulled JV out of his thoughts. The men had stopped.

Scolding himself for his inattention, JV darted behind a tree and pressed his back against the bark. He held his breath and waited, not daring to move until there was a sign that the immediate threat of detection had passed.

Neither man spoke for what seemed like forever. Then Stocky's voice broke the silence.

"Well, I'm not saying you imagined it, eh, but I don't hear anything strange. Relax a little bit, man. Remember that plenty, plenty animals run around this forest."

JV waited another few seconds and then peeked around the trunk. Cutlass was peering at something on the bark of a sandalwood tree but he didn't linger for long before giving a quick signal that they were moving on.

JV hung back and kept a closer eye on the two men. Curious as to what had caught Cutlass's interest, however, he took a look at the sandalwood as he passed. At first glance, he didn't notice anything unusual, but after leaning in closer, he smiled broadly at the sight of a small reflective tack pushed securely into the bark. They had marked the trail! He wouldn't have too much difficulty finding his way out, after all.

Through dips and hollows, flat land, and inclines, JV followed them. Checking his watch, he realised that almost forty minutes had passed since he had left the glade and he wondered how much longer the hike was going to take. Rain was predicted for later that afternoon, and he would need to be out of the forest by then. Sidestepping an especially muddy patch of earth, he pushed away some enormous elephant ears that grew from stalks as tall as he was, impeding his view of what was going on up ahead, and then froze. Not too far off was a crudely constructed wooden hut camouflaged with leaves, packed soil, and twigs, and Cutlass and Stocky were heading right toward it. The trek, it seemed, was over.

The two men disappeared inside, shutting the door behind them, and JV hesitated for a minute, debating whether he should risk moving any closer. High above the forest roof, dark clouds began to gather. JV considered his options. The guys looked like they meant serious business, and who knew what they would do to him if he got caught. But at the same time, it would be a terrible shame to have come all this way and leave none the wiser about what was going on in that hut. Curiosity won out over reason.

He inched forward, crouching, trying to stay hidden from view beneath low-lying plants which provided excellent cover. He didn't stop until he had crept all the way up to the side of the structure. Carefully removing a layer of leaves from a small spot on the frame, he found a gap between two planks and, pressing his face against the musty wood, squinted through the narrow slit. His nose was immediately accosted by a putrid stench, but it was his eyes that were absolutely horrified by what they saw.

The opposite and back walls of the hut were lined with metal cages, stacked one on top of the other and crammed with parrots, toucans, macaws, finches, iguanas, terrapins, and monkeys. And in other enclosures, additionally secured with panels of glass, JV could see coils and knots of snakes of varying colours, lengths, and sizes. He guessed that there must have been hundreds of creatures under that one thatched roof.

Cutlass and Stocky stood close to the door, their sacks resting on the ground at their feet. They were speaking with a man whose full black beard could not mask the hard, mean face beneath. He sat on a stool, his back against a cage of finches and his feet propped up on a cardboard box on the floor. A half-empty bottle of an amber-coloured liquid stood within easy reach of the short, stubby fingers of his dangling right hand.

"Where's Jacobs?" Stocky asked.

"He's gone to firm up transport plans," the bearded guy replied. "We won't see him back here until tonight." He massaged his temples, pulled a silver card of tablets from his breast pocket, and popped a few of the pills in his mouth. "I'll tell you something, though," he said. "I can't wait until this shipment is gone. I've had a stinkin' migraine since the start, and if I have to listen to these lousy animals for one more day than necessary...let's just say all the merchandise won't get to the destination in one piece." He turned around and gave the finch cage a violent shake, making the birds flutter wildly.

"And that fella over there?" he continued, pointing toward the back corner that wasn't within JV's range of vision. "He's no company at all, at all. Wouldn't even take a drink with me. He'd rather sneak food to these critters when he thinks I'm not looking." He reached down for the bottle and took a swig. "Anyhow," he said, swallowing hard. "How did it go with you two?"

Cutlass was the first to respond. "Not too bad."

"Yeah? Well, what happened to your neck, then?"

"Ran into one that had too much fight in him, but nothing I couldn't handle. Had to give him a double shot, though," he sneered, regarding the nearer of the two sacks and aiming a contemptuous kick at the lump within.

"Hey! Watch the merchandise," Migraine shouted. "Any cut in profit I'm taking out of your share."

With fists clenched, Cutlass stepped forward, scowling. Migraine stood and kicked the cardboard box, sending it skittering off to the side. The two men glared at each

89

other and JV wondered who would throw the first punch. But then Cutlass, without saying a word, stooped to untie the sack. He reached in and yanked out the limp body of a capuchin monkey—its head lolling to the side and slack jaws hanging open. He handed the wretched specimen to Migraine, who held it up by the neck fur, twirling it around slowly for a closer examination.

"What's this? No tail? What good is he?"

JV's eyes widened. *Oh no! They have Curty.* He pressed his face even tighter against the wooden planks.

"Who would want a monkey with no tail?" Migraine was shouting.

"That's what I said," Stocky piped up.

"Look, I couldn't see he had no tail when I shot the first dart," Cutlass said testily. "And when I realised, he had already given me so much trouble that I figured we could still get a price for him. If not," he added, looking at the monkey with unmistakable loathing, "he'll be easy enough to get rid of."

Migraine shook his head in disgust and practically threw Curty back to Cutlass, who promptly stuffed him in an empty cage. Stocky held up two other tranquillised capuchins that had been in the second sack. After a quick nod from Migraine, he added them to the cage and slammed the gate shut.

The hair on the back of JV's neck stood up. It may have been the terrible scene that was playing out in front of him, the thought of Curty coming to harm at the hands of these monsters, or the creeping feeling he was being watched. But unsettling as it was—and whatever its cause—he tried to shake it off and focus on what was happening through the crack. Migraine was now facing the back wall.

"And you? How's your work coming along back there?" he asked. "If you'd spend more time working and less worrying about the stupid animals, things would go a lot faster. Come on. Come closer. Bring it and lemme see."

There was an audible sigh, the thump of something heavy hitting the ground, and then the sight of a figure walking into view—a familiar figure—long legs, muscular arms, a prominent Adam's apple in a thin neck that held up a well-proportioned and handsome head. JV clamped his hand over his mouth just in time to stop the gasp of shock. Standing before his eyes, holding out an elaborate and sophisticated trap, was Mason De Couteau.

Chapter 8

Flight and Fright

"I think it stopped," JV said hopefully as he looked up at the sky through the kitchen window, his head bent as far back as his neck would allow.

"Mmm-hmm" was Granny B's non-committal response. She didn't bother to lift her eyes from her breakfast this time but kept right on picking at the last bit of speckled shell on her hard-boiled egg. It had been JV's third attempt to convince her that it was no longer drizzling and that it would be safe for him to go about his business without running the risk of catching pneumonia.

"Let's give it a little while longer just to make sure," she suggested, cutting through the now-naked egg's smooth white surface.

JV sighed. Yesterday, after the shock of seeing Mason, he had hastily patted the leaves and earth into place over the gap in the hut's wall and made his way back to the elephant ears, holding a crouched position until he was sure that the hut and all its horrors were behind him. Then he had straightened up and run, vowing under his breath that he would return to free the animals and get to the bottom of whatever it was that Mason was involved in. The wind, whistling through the leaves, had picked up, and the clouds had burst, but JV had escaped the worst of the rain. By the time it had begun to drum down on him he was clear of the forest and almost home. Even so, Granny B had met him at the door, wrapped a towel around his head, and instructed him to get out of his wet clothes. She made him take a steaming hot bath while she prepared a mug of chadon beni tea. He had dutifully complied, drunk the bitter brew without complaint, and graciously borne all her other attentions aimed at staving off a potential cold, just so he wouldn't be kept at home the next day.

Nonetheless, here he was, still stuck at home waiting for the barely there, fine sprinkles of rain to stop floating down. Somehow, this did not fit in with his grand idea of swooping into Oscuros like a hero to save the animals.

Irked by the delay, JV turned away from the window and stifled a yawn. He had not slept well and for a moment considered going back to bed. But he knew no matter how tired he was he wouldn't have any more luck getting restful sleep now than he had last night. There were just too many hurdles to overcome.

He would first have to shut out the images of those poor, confined creatures; then convince his mind to stop thinking about what lay in store for Curty if he didn't do something to help; and, on top of all that, he would need to put aside any thoughts of Mason, who was supposed to still be in Landing Town waiting for the floods to subside. *When exactly did he get back, and what role is he playing in the whole sordid operation? Should I tell Granny B about what I've seen? Or should I wait until I've scouted a bit more and at least tried to rescue the animals?* JV's head was full of questions.

And the impediments to peaceful slumber did not end there. The final snag was the horrible vision that came alive in vivid detail as soon as he closed his eyes: a nightmare of being trapped in a steel maze, running in circles, unable to follow the two sets of disappearing footprints that would lead him out, and being pursued by ghastly, salivating monsters intent on eating him alive. An involuntary shiver ran up his spine. Even thinking of the bad dream in the safety of the bright morning light gave him the chills. No, it would be useless to try to get any sleep.

He cast a glance at Kockot, preening herself in her cage, and immediately compared her to the animals he had seen in the hut. He had always thought of her as a merry bird that liked being in her little home in the kitchen, enjoyed the tasty morsels that she was given, basked in his grandmother's tender loving care, and chirped gaily to communicate her overall contentment. But now, for the first time in the four years that she had been with them, JV wondered whether Kockot was happy after all, whether she perceived her cage for the prison it truly was, and if her chirps were really trying to convey love or resentment, delight or despair.

"Granny?" he asked after spending a few moments in thought.

"Yes, Jason?"

"Isn't it wrong to keep Kockot in a cage?"

She looked up at her bird, which was pecking at some seeds and bits of carrot in the half-empty food tin.

"Wrong?" she said in a tone that to JV sounded both hurt and defensive. "Why should it be wrong? She's my companion, and I take good care of her. Search high, search low, you won't find a bird who is better treated on this island." She rested down her mug, reached over, and poked a wrinkled brown finger through the bars, wagging it up and down. "Isn't that right, my little spoiled fish?" The parakeet nipped at the intruding finger and then went back to the contents of her tin.

"Yes, but how do you know she doesn't want to be let out?" JV asked.

"But Jason, what are you really saying? You know she spends time outside her cage every day: on my shoulder, on the windowsill, even on the counters...when they're clean." Granny B dismissed the cluttered surfaces with a sweep of her hand.

"I know, I know," JV responded impatiently. "I don't mean let her out for a little while and then put her back in the cage afterward, but set her free. For good."

Granny B took a sip from her mug before answering. "But where would she go, Jason? How would she manage all alone? You know we're the only family she has."

"But what if we're not?" JV pressed. "What if she was taken away from her nest and her real family—her bird family—and they're still waiting for her to come back?" He was thinking once again of all the creatures in the forest that had been seized by those awful men.

Granny B studied him carefully. "We're not really talking about Kockot, are we Jason?" She set down her mug.

"Well…" JV stalled.

Granny B stretched across the table and patted his hand. "It's all right, Jason," she said. "I have a mind I know where this is coming from. You're still thinking about your parents and wondering where they might be and if anyone out there is looking for you. Am I right?"

"Um…"

"You don't have to explain, son. Just know I'm here if you need me to listen." She gave his hand a gentle squeeze and then turned toward the window. "Oh! Look at that. The drizzle has really stopped this time." She pushed her chair back, got up, and took her dishes over to the sink. "Well, go on, then. I know you're anxious to rush into Oscuros. But just do me a favour and keep an eye out for the rain this time, please."

It wasn't often that Granny B didn't get it right when it came to reading people or situations. Of course JV had questions about the identity of his parents and the circumstances that led to his abandonment, but he had no answers—yet—and the situation with the caged animals in the forest was urgent. Part of him wanted to open up to Granny B about everything he had seen, but he was also glad that she had missed the mark this once. The misunderstanding saved him quite a bit of explaining.

"OK, Granny," he said, almost knocking over his chair as he jumped up. He practically ran to the doorway, only turning around briefly to give Kockot a quick parting look. *That conversation with Granny B will have to wait until another time,* he thought. Right now, he needed to put his mind to work to come up with some sort of rescue plan. He exited the kitchen, hopped down the porch steps, and crossed the yard in the direction of the forest.

❀ ❀ ❀

It was truly a fine day under the trees of Oscuros. The scattered rays of light that penetrated the leafy roof had a crisp, unsullied quality to them, giving the forest interior an almost golden glow, and the warmth from the overhead canopy, together with the cool drafts that playfully wove themselves among the lively leaves and branches, conspired to bring about nothing less than an optimal temperature. It was an ideal balance that JV would have enjoyed had he not been intensely focused on devising a plot to free Curty and the other captives. He had hoped that a brilliant idea would have come to him by now, but no matter what plan he thought of, it was difficult to get past the unfair odds of four baddies—five, if he included Mason—against one pre-adolescent hero.

"There must be some way you can do this on your own, JV," he muttered, tramping along. He knew his way to the little clearing almost by heart now and was just about to dodge the low-hanging branch when the skin on his forearms began to tingle and erupted in a dense layer of goose bumps that made his kinky wisps of hair stand straight up to attention. It was that feeling again. Of being watched, but not quite like when he was outside the hut. This time the perception was more acute…and unmistakable. It was as though he could actually feel eyes boring into his back, his neck, and his head—alert, unblinking eyes tracking every move he made.

Remaining crouched, he swivelled slowly and scanned the trees. Although he did not see anything out of the ordinary, the lack of visible proof of a stalker only heightened his concern. Who—or what—he was dealing with was extraordinarily stealthy and his surroundings were putting him at a major disadvantage. Hadn't he himself proven how easy it was to hide among these trees and give pursuit without being detected?

JV realised that if he wanted to have any sort of chance, he needed to get to the clearing—and fast. He scurried under and past the branch and then took off running, suppressing as he did so, the urge to look back at his pursuer.

Trunks and branches flew by in a blur, and leaves whipped at his cheeks as he sped along. Thankfully, he didn't have too much farther to go. The final line of trees that stood at the fringe of the clearing was just visible up ahead. Then, in his haste, his foot caught on some unseen obstruction. He grabbed a branch and managed to avoid a fall, but the stumble slowed him down. He was now certain he could hear movement close behind. His heart fought wildly against the confines of his narrow chest, like a cornered beast.

For an instant, he was overcome with fear. This was it. This was how the short life of Jason Felix Theodore Valentine ended. He would be caught, murdered, and probably eaten. Never to be heard from again. And parents would tell their children his story to make sure they stayed away from Oscuros.

The thought of such a horrific death spurred him on and with a final burst of adrenaline, he pushed through the last set of branches and into the clearing. Panting heavily from exertion and fear, he turned around to face the trees that had engulfed him moments before and carefully backed up toward the centre of the glade.

At first, the rustling was almost imperceptible. Then the crunch and snap of wood became clearly audible. Paralysed with fright, JV kept his eyes trained on the spot where he had emerged seconds before. He could detect nothing at first but then he noticed movement. It was impossible, but it seemed that the stand of trees was getting closer and closer. Was it actually closing in on him? Had he lost his mind? Either way, he was in trouble.

With arms trembling at his sides, he watched in wide-eyed horror as a form seemed to detach itself from the wider backdrop of foliage and step forward. It was the product of such a bizarre mix of traits that JV's brain could not categorize it right away as plant or animal, beast or man. It was quite simply the most unnatural sight that he had ever beheld.

The being stood on two thick, powerful legs that tapered down to end in tough, charcoal-black hooves. In sharp contrast, its upper body was like that of a man with a broad chest, chiselled abdominals, muscular arms, and large hands. Even the head and face bore human-like features, barring the two short, pointy horns on the crown. The unearthly entity's body was covered in a thick olive-green layer of what appeared to be a combination of moss and fur that grew longer and denser on its cheeks and chin, creating a shaggy beard that fell all the way to its waist. The creature's only ornament was a large, curved ram's horn, which hung from a sturdy cord about its neck and sat squarely in the middle of its chest on top of the beard.

JV, able to think of nothing other than escape, unsuccessfully willed his feet to take another step backward. With a swift and agile leap, the fiend closed the distance between them and planted itself directly before JV. It smelled of earth and rain, of pine and musk, and being so close, JV could now see that its beard, swaying inches away from his nose, was matted with leaves. Recognising that any hope of flight was unrealistic, he stood perfectly still with fists clenched and eyes squeezed shut while the creature circled him slowly.

Steeling himself for the imminent attack, JV bid a silent farewell to Granny B and only hoped that the last stage in this tragic situation would be quick and relatively painless. Then, just as he was considering the various means that his captor could employ to bring about his end, a deep, gravelly voice commanded, "Raise your lids, Man's child."

Unwilling to run the risk of making things worse for himself by not cooperating, JV opened his eyes and saw that the being was standing a little farther away than before. It was regarding him sternly with its arms crossed over its chest, just below the ram's horn.

"You," it stated in a tone that hinted of recognition, and in that instant JV's terror collided with bewilderment. He was certain that he had not had any previous encounter with this creature. "State why you have come, Man's child," it commanded. "What is your business among these trees?"

"A-a-animals," JV stammered quickly. "In cages." Given his state of dread, it was the best answer that he could manage. No sooner had the words been uttered than his inquisitor pawed at the ground with its right hoof, took a menacing step forward, and looked on him with dark, unblinking eyes.

"And what have you to do with these…cages, Man's child?" it asked in a low growl. Sensing the savage fury that was only barely being kept in check, JV quailed as he tried to get out his next reply.

"N-n-nothing. I mean, my friend C-c-curty is trapped, and...and all the others too...and, well...the cages...I have to open the cages to let them out." Sweat trickled down his back and legs, and he began to wonder what would eventually do him in: the creature, his own fear, or the mental and emotional toll it was taking to answer these questions.

The dark eyes studied JV at length and the stern, threatening expression that had been fixed on him up to that moment seemed to soften. The being brought a large hand to its chin and stroked at the long beard.

"Friend, you say," it mused. The boy nodded vigorously and the creature paced back and forth, its hooves making a soft, clopping thud as they hit the earth. A few more steps and the pacing came to a halt. JV gulped. He sensed that the creature had reached a decision about him. The final moment had arrived.

"Come, Man's child!" the creature ordered.

On tremulous legs and with his heart pounding frantically in his throat, JV approached the creature with as much courage as he could muster. But he couldn't avoid casting down his eyes when his assessor scrutinised him once more before clearing its throat and continuing.

"Listen well, Man's child. Wisdom follows. I am Papa Bois. Master of this domain. My companion and I are protectors of the forest children: plants and animals alike. We defend our charges against Man's sons and daughters who seek to do them harm with orange tongues that burn, sharpened ores that cut, biting teeth that crush... and cages that trap. I am as old as this earth." It gently pawed at the ground again. "Your race, Man's child, savagely abuses nature's gifts of food and shelter, greedily appropriates and destroys them, and gives free reign to its insatiable appetites and unquenchable thirsts." The deep voice rumbled before continuing in a softer tone. "There must be balance or ruination is sure to follow." He paused, perhaps considering his own words and envisioning what such a world would be like.

JV was speechless. Papa Bois was real, after all. He thought of the stories, the tales that had been accompanied by lessons to respect nature, and saw how accurate the descriptions of the legendary protector had been. Yet JV still hadn't recognised him. He supposed that for him all those stories had been just that—traditional tales— and he never thought that he, Jason Valentine, would ever have a run-in with Papa Bois himself.

"But you, Man's child—you are different," Papa Bois continued. "I have watched you roam through my domain, and you have done no harm. I have also heard you take a vow: a noble vow that my messenger, the wind, carried to each end of my dominion. A vow made in the forest, Man's child, is unbreakable, and I am here to ensure that it is honoured. Now, tell me. How thought you to deliver my charges from their misfortune?"

For a moment, JV couldn't respond. It appeared that he was going to live after all. Taut muscles throughout his body relaxed just a little, and his heart rate took its first beat toward a return to normalcy. Then he recalled that he had no plan.

"Well, Man's child?" Papa Bois asked impatiently.

"Um...I was thinking of waiting until there were only two or three bad guys in the hut and then creating a diversion so that they'd come running out and I could slip in."

Papa Bois seemed unconvinced.

"What diversion?" he asked.

"I didn't really—"

"Humph!" said Papa Bois. "Your plan is weak, Man's child. But tell me this: How many more of Man's sons and daughters will be aiding you with this duty?"

"None," JV said simply. "It's just me. But I can do it." Suddenly, though, he felt foolish. Papa Bois was regarding him with what looked suspiciously like amusement.

"Aah...," the Protector remarked knowingly. "I should have suspected as much from one of your species. But still, it is fascinating to find such pride and confidence in one so young. Listen well, Man's child. Wisdom follows. Remember that it does not take one but two hands to clap. What is impossible alone often only requires assistance to be feasible. Even I, Papa Bois, have help." The Protector's gaze left JV's face and turned toward the trees behind the pond.

JV bit his lip. His mind raced. Papa Bois was distracted and JV could use this as an opportunity to escape. Then he considered his chances of outrunning the master of the forest and quickly calculated that they were zero to none. What's more, there probably weren't very many who had dared defy Papa Bois and had lived to speak of it. With that sobering thought, he tightened his fists and steeled his nerves in anticipation of whatever it was the Protector was awaiting.

Chapter 9

The Pact

JV cautiously drew alongside Papa Bois. He followed the Protector's gaze and stared past the pond but could see nothing to explain the forest guardian's vigilance. Bewildered, he looked up, past lively strands in a beard that was being tugged at by the wind, past the smooth ram's horn, and finally fixed on the broad, inscrutable face focused directly ahead. He then caught the slow, deliberate movement of one of Papa Bois's long, hairy arms as it rose, unfurling a thick finger as it did so, a finger that pointed toward the trees before them. Too short to see the object of such attention and growing increasingly apprehensive, JV took a discreet step closer to the sturdy frame at his side. He was by no means comfortable being this close to Papa Bois, but as Granny B had said time and time again, "better the devil you know than the devil you don't."

Although his eyes were riveted to the spot indicated by Papa Bois's finger, JV didn't detect anything unusual right away. He soon heard the rustle of leaves and crack of twigs. With teeth clenched, he prepared himself for what he was sure would be the emergence of another frightful character: perhaps a lagahoo not yet morphed back into the shape of a man, or maybe even La Diablesse with her frilly petticoats and cloven hoof coming to take him away. A day ago such thoughts would have been laughable, but nothing much that could step from behind those trees today would surprise JV. His musings were cut short when Papa Bois, with finger still held aloft, finally spoke.

"My companion and co-protector: Mama D'Lo."

A figure approached, advancing closer and closer, its form becoming less blurry with each step until— oh!— JV was indeed caught by surprise. Circling the pond and coming toward them, indisputably real and now close enough to touch, was the mysterious lady he had seen in that same place almost a week before. She was of regular height, and the deep hue of her skin, which created a striking contrast with the colour of her eyes, seemed to glow. Her dark, braided locks twisted down, their ends brushing the waist of a patterned dress of rippling green, brown, and gold scales that fell to the forest floor. Her presence alone would have been shock enough but, following just behind, cradling a small ball of fur from which protruded a snout and a pink whip-like tail, was Adelle De Couteau. Head bowed over the squirming animal, little Adelle sang softly and caressed its soft coat, her strokes uninterrupted even as the lady's slender fingers guided her forward.

With a coy smile, the beautiful woman glided up to JV, who, dumbfounded, remained rooted to the spot. She looked him up and down, studying him at length, though her face did not betray any sign of recognition.

"Is this the one?" she finally asked Papa Bois, never taking her eyes off of JV.

"It is," the Protector said. "He is as I thought him to be. He will do."

The lady bestowed another enchanting smile on JV.

Papa Bois focused on the tiny ball in Adelle's hands.

"Yet another foundling, Mama?" he asked, peering at the restless creature.

"Sadly, yes. This opossum's parents are nowhere to be found, but we're doing a good job with her. Aren't we, little one?"

Without missing a note in her song, Adelle looked up and gave the faintest of nods before once again directing her undivided attention to her charge.

"My little friend, my forest friend,
There's nothing to fear from me;
I'll keep you safe and warm and fed,
All shall be well, you'll see.
My little friend, my forest friend,
Don't worry you're not alone;
Though you may be hurt, feel lost and scared,
With me you have a home."

JV snapped out of his stupor. Something wasn't right. Adelle had seen him—he was sure of it—but it was as though she had looked right through, and then past, his body. Her big brown eyes, so much like her mother's, were blank.

"Adelle!" he called out. "It's me, JV. Jason Valentine." But she simply stood where she was, chin to chest, humming and tenderly stroking the now subdued creature. Taking a step toward her, he tried again, struggling to keep the panic from his voice even as a cold feeling of dread threatened to overwhelm him.

"Adelle! Adelle De Couteau! It's time to go home now. Everyone has been looking for you. Your parents are worried sick." He reached out and grasped her by the wrist, but she did not react and her humming did not stop. Instead, it was Papa Bois who spoke.

"She will not answer, Man's child."

The way that he said it—in a calm, matter-of-fact sort of way—only heightened JV's alarm. He tightened his grip around Adelle's thin wrist but got no response. *What is wrong with her? Why is she just standing there humming?* he thought.

"I have to get her back to the village," he murmured to himself. "She's not well."

"Not well, you say?" Papa Bois queried, bending over and inclining a horned head toward Adelle. Concern was unmistakably etched in the creased brow.

"Oh, she's just fine, Papa," Mama D'Lo reassured soothingly, gliding right up and brushing her fingers against the girl's cheeks. "Nothing is wrong with the child. I believe what the young man means is that—Adelle, is it?—yes, Adelle is different from how he remembers her. Isn't that right?" She turned to JV for confirmation, and he nodded solemnly.

"Ah yes…" Papa Bois conceded, straightening up, the lines on his forehead disappearing. "But that is to be expected. Worry not, Man's child. She will be as she was, once my vow has been fulfilled."

JV's eyebrows shot up, and his voice rose. "Vow? You made a vow too? What sort of vow? And what's wrong with Adelle? What did you do to her?" His eyes darted from Papa Bois to Mama D'Lo, then back again to Papa Bois, and he momentarily released his grip on Adelle but only so he could place a protective arm around her shoulders to draw her closer.

"Come, come dear." Mama sighed. "Don't get upset. No harm has come to your friend. We are neither her foes nor yours. She is truly an innocent and will be restored. Although, that mostly depends on you."

"Me?" JV asked, truly bewildered.

"Yes, but I am not the one to explain," she said, moving away.

JV focused on the Protector.

"It is as Mama D'Lo has said it to be," Papa Bois confirmed, lowering his haunches to the earth and then crossing his long hoofed legs before him. Once settled, he gestured toward Adelle and began his tale.

"I first observed this youngling at the edge of my dominion. Timid, she dared not enter, though it was clear that the one for whom she waited and the intended recipient of what she bore was already within the forest realm. From the cover of the trees, I watched her wait until another Man's child, older and taller than yourself although not yet fully grown, emerged, met with her, and retrieved her burden. I believe you know of whom I speak." He paused. JV did know. It had to be Mason. He gave a brief nod, and Papa Bois continued.

"I watched the youngling turn toward the direction from whence she came, and I then followed the Man's child to an abominable lair where many of my forest charges were being held captive."

The Protector's eyes flashed angrily, and a deep growl rumbled in his throat, causing JV to pull Adelle even closer. There was no doubt as to what Papa Bois was capable of, and JV had visions of the hut's roof being torn off, the wooden walls crashing down, and vengeance and damnation being delivered on the captors inside.

111

"Yes, your instincts are right," Papa Bois said, watching JV carefully. "At that moment, I thought my rage knew no bounds and that I was capable of anything. But remember this, Man's child. Wisdom follows. Rage alone is no answer. I am no friend to those who wantonly kill and capture my charges and on occasion have paid them back in kind. But alas, in this instance—though I would eagerly take matters into my own hands—my passion and strength are of no use to me."

JV furrowed his brow. He did not understand how Papa Bois—as mighty as he was—could be so...well, powerless. If he knew about the animals in the hut, why didn't he just go in and rescue them? As if reading JV's thoughts, Papa Bois continued after gently brushing away a large horsefly that attempted to perch on his leathery nose.

"I understand your confusion, Man's child. Listen well. You see, the Protector and Co-protector's realm is the forest—a dominion created solely by Mother Nature—and the lair built by human hands is beyond our domain. So despite all my will and strength, I may not enter." He looked away, as though ashamed of this limitation, and JV immediately felt sorry for the half man, half beast who could not carry out his duty to protect his charges. Then he remembered Adelle.

"But what does that have to do with Adelle? Why is she like this?"

"I am getting to that."

JV waited impatiently while Papa Bois repositioned himself, now curling both legs under his haunches.

"So with impotent rage, I left that terrible place only to come across this youngling once again, the very same who not too long before had met with one of the captors of my charges. She was lying unmoving on the forest floor. Bending over her were three of those mischief-makers—those douens of the forest—who, despite my constant scolding, never tire of luring Man's children into my realm and getting them lost. Humph. It will be a fine day indeed when their little backward feet lead them and their straw hats far away from these trees. I do hope that you, Man's child, will be smarter than to ever succumb to their tricks and wiles."

JV had heard tales of douens. They were supposedly spirits of dead children that roamed the forests, enticing their living counterparts in with songs and games, only to abandon them once they were completely lost beneath the dark boughs. Given his present company, he certainly wasn't shocked to hear that they too were real. Suddenly Pascal's gibberish the afternoon before about straw hats and feet now made perfect sense. He and his sister must have had a run-in with these very douens. It definitely explained Carol's refusal to set another foot in Oscuros and her cryptic warning that JV should also stay away. Of course, it would have been nice if she'd been more specific, but if he were honest with himself it probably wouldn't have made a difference. Chances were he may not have believed her, or if he did, it would have just been one more compelling reason to rush into the forest.

"Ahem. As I was saying," Papa Bois said. "Though she was unconscious, life had not as yet left the youngling. I could still sense the tormented state of her mind. Blinded by my desire for revenge, I would have left her to her fate, but Mama D'Lo sent the douens on their way, and she said these words, which caused me to reconsider: 'She is but a young innocent. She herself has done nothing wrong. Her spirit is pure. I shall watch over her.' To which I replied, 'What you say may be so, but I in turn vow that her mind shall not completely awake from its slumber until every last one of my charges is free. Until such time she is yours to care for, as you so desire it.' And that, Man's child, is the irreversible vow I made."

JV turned to look at Adelle. Her demeanour had not changed—she was still in her own little world, humming and completely unaware of his presence.

"I have to take her back," he said for the second time, trying to guide the unresponsive child away, without success.

"You may do as you like," Papa Bois said. "But know that if she leaves the forest as she is, she will never again be the youngling you knew and will be forever lost to her parents. For the youngling to be restored, my vow must be fulfilled, and for that I require your help, Man's child. Remember your own vow to rescue my charges. I ask nothing of you that you yourself were not willing to do."

JV did not like the choice he had to make. The whole village had been looking for Adelle and had given up hope, and here she was standing next to him. She should be at home with her parents. Surely they would find a way to make her better. But deep down, JV knew that Papa Bois was right and that he couldn't take Adelle back to the village—not yet and not like that. He let his arm fall away from her shoulders, and Mama D'Lo, who had been waiting silently a few paces off, drifted over and took Adelle's hand in hers. She then reached out with her free hand and gently lifted JV's chin so that he was looking directly in her eyes. He hadn't noticed before, but up close he saw that her pupils were diamond-shaped.

"No harm shall come to her while she is in my care," she said, the words sliding into his ears. "You have my promise."

JV swallowed hard and, with difficulty, cast down his eyes. Mama D'Lo let go of him, said, "I will return shortly," and when he next looked up, she and Adelle were disappearing in the direction from which they had come. Once they had vanished, he turned to Papa Bois.

"So what now?" JV asked.

"We make plans for the rescue of my charges and carry them out." Papa Bois gestured toward a patch of mossy earth alongside him. "Sit," he said.

JV was aware of finally feeling more at ease in the Protector's company. He sat.

"Papa Bois?" he asked.

"Yes?"

"I have a question."

"And you may ask it, Man's child."

"Why do you wear a horn around your neck?"

"It is as good a place as any to keep it. And my charges heed me when I blow."

"May I hear it?"

"Its sound is not for human ears."

"Oh. Papa Bois?"

"Yes, Man's child?"

"I have another question."

"I thought you might. You may ask it."

"Can you tell me about Mama D'Lo?"

The chuckle that started deep in Papa Bois's chest escaped as a hearty laugh, resonating throughout the woods.

"Listen well, Man's child. Wisdom follows. Very little is as it first appears. Though she may not look it, Mama D'Lo is as old as I and every bit as powerful. The form you see is not one that you can trust." He grinned down at JV. "And know this. She has husbands enough in this life and the next, though she is always on the lookout for more." He chuckled again, and JV, feeling a little foolish, decided he would never ask about the beautiful lady again.

The sun had begun its slow descent, generously flecking everything with its copper rays. JV's eyes were drawn to the gleaming clusters of light on the pond's surface, and then to Mama D'Lo who now sat on one of the rocks along the bank. The shimmering skirt of her dress fanned out and its back flowed into the water. Adelle was not with her. Perhaps sensing JV's concern, Mama D'Lo gave him a slight nod and said, "As promised, she is well."

The three then started crafting a rescue plan. By the end of the discussion, however, JV was still worried. This was no game, and he would be in danger. Would all go as they had devised? The fates of Adelle and Curty, and his own safety depended on it. Was he really up to a mission of such great importance?

Unwilling to admit to such insecurities, JV kept those doubts to himself. The Protector bade him a sober good-bye before disappearing through the trees, and Mama D'Lo gave him a parting smile as she slipped off the rock and into the water. Whether he was ready or not, the time for action had come. JV cast aside his reservations and ran off to execute the plan.

Chapter 10

Danger, Danger Everywhere

JV crouched behind the elephant ears once more and kept a close eye on the hut. He had been in position for ten minutes but had seen no one enter or leave. Not sure how long he would have to wait, he was about to give his knees a rest and sit when he saw the door open. Stocky came out, stretched his arms, and leaned against the wall.

"Kis-ka-dee! Kis-ka-dee!" JV called, mimicking the song of the small bird of the same name.

He did not have to wait long for the plan to unfold. Stocky stepped away from the hut and leaned forward. He craned his neck to get a better look into the tall grass in front of him. Then he froze. He remained that way for a few seconds before backing away. He bumped into the door, turned, and scurried inside.

JV stayed low and snuck closer. He heard shouts and could distinguish the words 'anaconda,' 'just outside,' and 'hurry.' His location, well hidden by the surrounding foliage, provided an excellent view of the front of the hut and he watched as Stocky rushed out of the door, his rifle trained on the forest floor. Cutlass and Migraine followed close behind, their weapons dangling casually at their sides. Mason emerged last, hanging back with his arms crossed.

"I'm telling you that anaconda is somewhere close," Stocky shouted, the thick carpet of leaves crunching loudly each time he took a step forward.

"Now listen here," Migraine snarled, stopping short. "I have the day planned out good, good. We have no time to waste on this stupidness, you hear? Jacobs will be back soon with the transport, and we still have to get the animals ready to travel to the gulf today."

JV saw Migraine reach into his breast pocket.

"Look," Migraine said, waving a piece of paper in Stocky's face. "You see all these people waiting for the merchandise? If you think I'm bad, you haven't seen bad yet, and you can bet they won't put up with any delays,

119

especially over a phantom snake." He poked the list back into his shirt.

"Boss man, please," Stocky begged. "I know what I saw. I never thought a snake could get so big, but trust and believe—the shipment's worth two, three times more with it. I promise. All those buyers will be fighting over the tail alone." Migraine sucked his teeth, but Stocky ploughed ahead. "Give me half hour boss, and we'll have it. If not, you fellas can tie me up and put me on the boat instead." Stocky chuckled and then squirmed beneath his boss's glare. After a moment of silence, Migraine yielded.

"All right, start tracking your snake, but we're back here in twenty minutes—with or without it. Now, let's move."

Stocky straightened, readjusted his stun gun, and marched off, leading the others into the surrounding forest.

JV knew he didn't have much time before they, or the other guy—Jacobs—returned, so slipping from behind his leafy cover, he set off at full speed for the cabin.

Once he made it to the camouflaged wall, he did as he had on his last visit. He scratched away a section of mud and leaves to expose a gap between the wooden planks. Peering through, he allowed his eyes to adjust to the darkness within.

Everything was as it had been before, except that as far as he could tell no one was inside keeping watch over the miserable animals. And miserable they were, indeed. As if resigned to their unhappy circumstances, they seemed to have lost whatever fight they might have had when they were brought in and now waited listlessly. Motivated more than ever to get them out of there, JV crept along the wall until he reached the heavy door. It creaked open easily with a gentle push from his shoulder.

On entering the gloomy space, he braced himself against impact, half expecting to be tackled by some unseen form, and fearing that his mission would be brought to an end before it had actually begun. No attack came. There was no one else in the hut. Reassured, he walked in and immediately began searching for Curty. His little friend needed to be among the first ones to be released.

Hurrying along, he started to panic. He passed pythons and boa constrictors in their reinforced glass boxes, towering, compact cages of iguanas, turtles, parrots, finches, owls, and spider monkeys. Where were the capuchins? Wondering if by chance he had overlooked them in his haste or if they had already been removed, he tried to keep his discouragement at bay as he neared the back of the hut. But no luck there, either. Only a cage of uncommonly quiet caiques, followed by another cage with white hawks and then...could it be? Yes. There they were: three capuchin monkeys in the very last cage, and his buddy was among them!

JV ran up and undid the latch. Curty crawled forward and then sprang to his rescuer, clasping his wiry arms tightly about the boy's neck. As relieved and overjoyed as JV was, he was even more conscious of the passing time and all that was yet to be done. He gently disengaged himself from the monkey's nimble fingers and said, "Go on and get out of here, Curty. Hurry! I've got a lot to do before those guys come back."

Curty briefly rested a hand on JV's chest, over his heart, then scampered off and disappeared out the door. When he was gone, JV looked down at the open cage. The other two capuchins were still huddled together, cowering in the rear corner.

"Come on, you're free. Move it," he urged, trying to coax them out. But they shrank back from his outstretched hand and refused to leave.

"Aw, come on. We don't have much time," he pleaded again. They didn't budge. Recognising that he had hit a brick wall with those two, JV was about to move on to the hawks in the next cage when he heard voices approaching.

"Uh-oh," he moaned. "Here they come. Sorry, guys!" he whispered, and hastily closed the door on the terrified monkeys.

Whirling around, he frantically scanned the room for a place to hide. There was practically no furniture apart from the one small stool and a few cardboard boxes that served as tables. No help there. The voices were louder now, and he could clearly catch what they were saying. Migraine sounded furious.

"Waste of time! Should have known better than to follow that fool. He better find his way back here pronto or—which one of you two idiots left the door wide open?"

"Don't look at me. Young boy was the last one out." JV recognised that voice as belonging to Cutlass.

"You left the door open, boy?"

"I...I don't know...I can't remember... I don't think so..."

"Steups. How can I fly with eagles when I'm working with turkeys, eh? Tell me that. You better hope all's in order."

JV finally zeroed in on an untidy pile of tarps in the corner. He dashed toward it, squatted down, and pulled one of the huge canvas sheets over his head just as the first set of footsteps entered the cabin. There, in the darkness, his eyes were drawn to a small circle of light. Readjusting his body ever so slightly, he was able to peep through a hole that was no bigger than the width of his index finger. Through it he saw that Migraine, Cutlass, and Mason had returned and were looking around.

"You're lucky," Migraine said to Mason as he cast an eye about the hut. "It could've turned out badly for you." He snapped his fingers. "Let's get to work."

They propped the guns and blades against the front wall and picked up rolls of tape that were resting on one of the makeshift tables. Each then headed to a cage that was crammed with birds and, releasing the latches, began to bind their beaks shut.

Work progressed smoothly at first. Then it was as though an invisible switch had been flicked. Without warning, the orderly scene of a fraction of a second before was inexplicably replaced by one of utter chaos. The birds flapped and fluttered wildly, and those whose beaks had not yet been sealed let out earsplitting shrieks; monkeys grabbed and shook the bars of their cages, hooting and screaming; tangles of hissing snakes writhed in a frenzy, their heads thumping against the glass enclosures; and iguanas scurried around their meshed confines, whipping their tails from side to side. Initially, JV was as baffled by the animals' behaviour as the men he was watching seemed to be, but then he understood: this was Papa Bois's doing. The Protector had launched the second part of their plan, using his horn to call the animals to rise up and fight.

"What in the world—" Migraine began, but a spectacled owl that he had been clumsily attempting to subdue pecked fiercely at his palm, and his exclamation ended in a yelp of pain. He slammed the cage door shut and cradled the injured hand against his chest. Cutlass and Mason quickly followed suit, closing the cages they had opened and regarding each other in confusion. Then Migraine roared hoarsely above the infernal racket.

"Be quiet!" he shouted over and over again. "Just shut up!" His eyes were squeezed closed and he was massaging his temples. Pain was plastered all over his face. Cutlass and Mason practically jumped out of their boots when Migraine turned on them.

"Stop standing there like idiots! What y'all waiting for? For my head to explode? You!" He grimaced, pointing at Cutlass. "Start tranquillising these beasts. Pump them full if you have to. I don't wanna hear another peep from these wretches for the rest of the day. And you," he said, addressing Mason, "go find that idiot and tell him to forget the stupid anaconda. We need him back here NOW! I'll be sure to deal with him when this job is over." Fumbling in his breast pocket, he pulled out his card of tablets and staggered to the door. "I'm gonna keep a lookout for Jacobs. Go on. Get going!"

Mason slipped past him then raced out, and Cutlass headed for the weapons against the wall.

✹✹✹

JV watched Cutlass grab a pistol along with some darts from the weapons stash near the door, load the gun, clip extra darts to his belt, and study the wall of rattling cages. Cutlass fingered the scratch on his neck, and then, with a bounce in his step, started toward the back of the hut where JV was hiding. JV's stomach tightened. He held his breath. Cutlass headed straight for the capuchins, strutted up to the cage, smirked, and looked in. His eyes widened and his mouth fell open. He reached for the cage door only to discover that it was unlatched.

"Bravo, little monkey" JV heard him mutter. "But if you weren't clever enough to make it outside, your days are numbered!"

Having secured the latch, Cutlass began a frenzied search, pulling cages away from the walls, upending boxes, and staring up at the spaces between the wooden rafters and the palm ceiling.

JV was sweating under the layers of canvas. There were only so many places for Cutlass to search in the tiny hut. It was just a matter of time before he was discovered. He needed to be ready.

Cutlass kicked the stool, and JV instinctively shut his eyes when it crashed to the ground. When he opened them Cutlass was no longer in his line of sight. JV listened closely. He did not have to wait long before he heard them—footsteps coming his way. He balled his hands into fists, preparing for the inevitable, and told himself that it was all about being quick enough to make it to the door. He had no doubt that Papa Bois would keep him safe once he escaped into the forest.

Any second now. Three...two...one...and whoosh! The tarps flew off with sudden force and the face before him registered hatred, bafflement, and fury. JV jumped out of reach and began his sprint toward freedom.

Running past the cages, he zigged and zagged to avoid the hands that swiped at him but kept his eyes focused on the door. He was almost there, stretching out to pull it open when two heavy hands clamped down on his shoulders and then pushed him chest-first on to the hard, dusty floor. He grimaced in pain as his wrists absorbed the shock of the fall and then he quickly flipped over so he could use his feet and rear end to scoot backward.

Cutlass spat to the side and then grinned down at him.

"So what do we have here?" he jeered, moving forward each time JV scooted back. "A troublemaker? A spy? A hero? Now let's see. You wouldn't happen to know the whereabouts of a certain tailless monkey, would you?"

JV could go no farther. His spine was up against the door.

"You see, I have a score to settle with him," Cutlass continued, "but he seems to have disappeared…which is too bad because someone else will have to pay."

As Cutlass lunged forward, JV reached up, grabbed a few darts from his attacker's belt, and plunged them deep into Cutlass's thigh. Letting out a loud bellow, Cutlass crumpled to the ground and pulled at the darts, trying to work them free while JV eased himself up bit by bit.

JV watched in shock as Cutlass's fingers slowly lost their dexterity—and finally stiffened into claws. The man's threats and curses, which had degenerated into gobble-dygook, were silenced. His chest still rose and fell, but whatever was in those darts had knocked him out cold. JV carefully stepped over him. He really had to hurry now. He had no idea how long the tranquillizers would last and he knew there was no way he'd be so lucky a second time if Cutlass woke up to find him still there.

He pushed the heavy body out of the way, pulled open the door, and then returned to his mission. The animals had calmed down. With heart pounding and adrenaline pumping, JV was about to liberate the first cage of scarlet macaws when the door to the cabin slammed shut.

"And exactly what do you think you're doing, little boy?" a gritty, menacing voice called out from behind him. JV despaired. He had no more fight left. Wearily, he turned to face what he bleakly assumed would be his final threat.

Chapter 11

Friend or Foe?

"You just couldn't stay away, could you?"

The eyes that met JV's were still sunken, sitting in deep, swollen pockets, but the rough stubble of six days ago had burgeoned into a full-grown beard, and Granny B's crisp white bandage was now a grubby grey-brown. As dishevelled as Mr. Phipps appeared, however, JV couldn't have been happier to see him.

"Thank goodness it's you!" JV exclaimed. "I definitely didn't have it in me to do that again." He pointed at Cutlass.

"What the…! How did you…? Is he…?" Two steps later, Phipps was stooping over the body feeling for a pulse.

"He isn't dead," JV said, looking on. "I already checked. But did you see all of this?" he asked, gesturing at the cages. "He and some others are planning to smuggle these animals out, and I've got to free them while there's still time. There're a lot of them though, so come on. Gimme a hand."

Phipps stood up, his eyes still taking in the man on the floor. "Where are his friends?"

JV recalled what he had heard while he was under the tarp. "One is looking for a guy who went after a snake, and the boss is outside waiting for someone else."

"Well, I don't know where the boss went, but he's not there now," Phipps said, looking troubled.

"Then that's good news," JV pointed out. "We have more time. Come on, we can do this."

But Phipps shook his head and crossed his arms. "Now listen here. You've gone and gotten yourself mixed up in something that doesn't concern you. But since I owe your granny a favour, I'll pretend I never saw you here. Just walk away and don't come back."

JV didn't move. He couldn't have heard Phipps correctly.

"Look, I'll make it even clearer," Phipps said. He pointed at the door and gestured for JV to go.

"No way. I can't leave without the animals."

"Well, we have a problem, because they're not going anywhere just yet."

129

JV finally caught on, and it felt like a powerful punch to the gut. Of course Mr. Phipps wouldn't help. He was one of the bad guys. He was most likely the man Migraine had been expecting.

JV stared at the stranger Granny B had welcomed into their house, who had eaten the lion's share of his favourite breakfast, and whose life they had probably saved. All he could think was that he had been right all along: the man should never have been trusted.

Disappointed and angry, he turned back to the macaws' cage. He still had a promise to keep and a job to do. But his fingertips had barely touched metal when Phipps's callused hands pulled him away and held him in an unyielding grip that only tightened the more he struggled.

"I'm not going to repeat myself, boy," Phipps said.

Just as JV was pondering his next move, pore-raising screams penetrated the hut from outside. Phipps jerked his head up and drew JV closer. Within seconds the screaming stopped and was followed by a deep, powerful voice that made the ground shake.

"It is Papa Bois before whom you cower," the voice thundered. "Protector of this domain and caretaker of its inhabitants, and it is I who ask what you want with my charges. You have captured, corralled, and mistreated the children of this forest, and I ask to what end?"

JV didn't know which criminal Papa Bois had caught but hoped it wasn't Mason. He tried to focus on this and not what action the Protector had taken to evoke such screaming.

"You do not answer?" the voice boomed again. "Well, more is the pity."

JV braced himself for more screams but none came. Phipps seemed unsure of what to do. He pulled JV with him toward the door, stopped and returned to where they had been standing. JV's mind was turning to how he was going to accomplish his task of freeing the animals when the door burst open. Wheezing and trembling violently, Mason ran past and went straight to the farthest end of the hut. He bent over, swallowing great gasping gulps of air. Then, as if struck by a burning thought, he straightened up, practically stumbled over himself to get back to the door, and quickly pushed it shut.

"Did you hear it, Jacobs?" he asked without turning around, as he checked and double-checked the door to make sure that it was properly closed. "Did you see it? A man-beast with horns."

"A what?" Phipps sputtered. "Were you the one screaming?"

"No, that wasn't me. But I heard them. The screams. And I saw it with my own eyes. A man-beast with horns!" Mason faced the room, and only then did he note JV's presence.

"What are you doing here?"

"I can ask you the same thing," JV shot back, renewing his battle against Phipps's arms. Mason jumped forward and tried to pry JV out of the hold.

"Hey, don't hurt him," Mason yelled. "He's only a kid."

131

"Just stopping him from making a big mistake, that's all. He thinks he's going to free the animals...but not today, he's not." Phipps gave JV an I'm-not-to-be-messed-with look of warning but loosened his grip and backed away from JV.

"Where's the snake hunter?" he asked Mason.

Mason shook his head. "I didn't see him. I ran for cover when I heard the screams and then saw that thing out there."

"Listen," Phipps said. "I don't know what's going on outside or what it is you saw, but I'm going to find the boss man. We need him and that shipping info for this thing to go down right. There's way too much at stake for things to go belly up now." He started for the door and then turned back. "Make sure you keep a good eye on this one until I get back and don't let him try any foolishness. See what he did over there?" He nodded toward Cutlass.

Mason took in the unconscious form and let out a slow whistle.

"Yeah, that's right," Phipps went on. "And I still don't know how he managed it, so watch out." He rushed from the cabin, and the two boys abruptly found themselves alone. JV rubbed his sore arms and eyed Mason with contempt.

"Well, you seem to be good at taking care of yourself," Mason finally said, glancing at Cutlass. "How'd you do it?"

"What are you doing here, Mason? How can you be a part of this?"

132

Mason hesitated and then, probably remembering his orders, stepped between JV and the cages. He lowered his eyes. "You know you can't free them, right?"

JV shook his head in disbelief. "Believe me, you'd want them out as much as I do if you understood what it meant."

"No, you're the one who doesn't understand," Mason countered. "You think I like this? You think I want to be here? There's a lot going on that you don't know."

"So why are you here, then? Everyone thinks you're in Landing Town. What about your internship?"

Mason waved JV off. "They gave it to someone else. But I needed the money—you know my dad isn't well and the stall took a hit from the drought—so when some guys asked me to build traps for them, I agreed. I didn't expected any of this," he said, looking at the cages. "All they told me was that they would be doing a little hunting, and I figured that some off-season trapping wasn't such a big deal. But they started going after protected animals, not just the usual game like agoutis, deer, and wild hogs. I tried to back out when I discovered what they were really up to but it was too late. And things have become more complicated."

"Why did you have to drag Adelle into it?"

"What do you mean?"

"Well, didn't she come to Oscuros to meet you?"

Mason looked closely at JV. "Yeah, but how did you know that?"

JV said nothing and remained stone-faced. Averting his eyes, Mason swallowed hard, and when he next spoke, it was obvious that he was struggling to maintain control of his unsteady voice.

"She followed me one day when I was supposed to be heading to football, but thankfully I realised just before getting to the forest. I didn't tell her what I was doing, only that it was really important and that no one could know as yet. She said she wanted to help too, that there must have been something she could do, even though she was small. So I told her I would be in the forest for a while." His lips trembled. "I said that she could bring me a few things like bread or biscuits on an afternoon while it was still bright. I made her promise that she would never leave the track or come in the forest and that she would head right back to the village afterward." He shook his head slowly. "The last time I saw her she brought me biscuits. She waved good-bye, turned around, and was making her way home." He finally broke down, his sobs mingling with the animal sounds around them. Uncomfortable, JV looked away.

"I've been searching for her since it happened, you know," Mason went on after a moment. "I even saw you in the forest that night when the whole village came out." JV thought back to the long night spent scouring Oscuros and remembered the lurking shadow behind the tree trunks.

"So what's happened since then?" Mason asked anxiously. "Has there been any news of her in the village?"

"Not yet," JV replied, "but…"

"But what?"

"I've seen her. And she's the reason I'm here. To help."

134

Mason's eyes immediately widened. "You've seen her?" he repeated. "Where? Is she OK?"

"She'll be all right," JV promised, "but only if we can get these animals out of here. You have to trust me."

The look on Mason's face turned fierce. "What are you talking about? What does this have to do with Adelle?"

"I'll explain, Mason, but not now," JV said. Too much time had already been wasted talking while the animals remained confined. "Help me or there won't be anything anyone can do for her."

Mason was silent for a second.

"If you're lying…" he warned, pointing a threatening finger at JV.

"You'll make sure I regret it?"

"Something like that."

❈ ❈ ❈

JV opened the last of the cages and stepped aside as the iguanas scrambled over each other in their haste to get out. Once free, a few scurried around, clearly disoriented, but most quickly found their way to the door and then out into the forest.

"So what about these?" Mason asked, looking at the snake enclosures.

"We have to push them outside and then open the lids a crack. Someone else will take it from there."

"Outside?" Mason gasped. "After what I saw out there? Forget it!"

"You'll be fine," JV said. "You're with me." When the rescue plan had been hatched, he had received Papa Bois's and Mama D'Lo's solemn promise that no harm would come to Adelle's brother as long as the older boy helped rescue the animals, and JV knew that he could trust the Protectors' word. "Besides," he continued, noticing that Mason looked unconvinced, "how're you going to see Adelle if you don't leave the hut?"

That did the trick. With a brief nod, Mason joined JV, and the two of them got to work lifting and pushing the glass boxes past the entrance to the cabin. They then slid the lids open and, retreating swiftly, left the scene just as forked pink and black tongues began to poke up into the fresh air.

❀❀❀

"So where exactly are we going? Will Adelle be there?" Mason's questions hadn't stopped since they'd left the hut. JV was doing his best to fill him in on everything as they hurried through the forest alongside a steadily broadening stream.

"I told you already, to a special place I found. The spot where I first saw Mama D'Lo. They said Adelle would be there."

"And you're sure Papa Bois won't hurt me?" I mean, from what I saw he's really scary…and angry."

"Oh, he's angry all right. But he said you'll be safe, and I trust him."

Mason kept up his questions: How did Adelle look when JV had seen her? How would Papa Bois know that the animals had been freed? How long would it take for Adelle's mind to be fully restored? How much longer before they got to where they were going? He was in the middle of asking another when he fell silent and stopped walking.

"What's wrong?" JV asked. He followed Mason's gaze and saw that up ahead, at a wide bend in the stream, Stocky was standing as still as stone, his rifle aimed at the water's edge. Neither boy moved or spoke.

Then JV saw Mama D'Lo. She seemed to gradually rise from the water, gently swaying rhythmically in a hypnotising dance that had clearly captivated Stocky. JV watched in stunned silence as she continued her slow rise and strained to hear when, on opening her mouth, she began to sing. Her voice was clear, the tone sweet, her lilt enchanting.

> "Another husband, another dear,
> Let me take you away from here.
> We shall be wed from now till then,
> For this life and the next again.
> One sweet embrace is all I need,
> One sweet embrace and your fate is sealed."

By this time, she was towering over the still-unresponsive Stocky, and JV, now seeing more of her than he had before, stifled the scream that threatened to escape his mouth. He glanced over and Mason's eyes were nearly falling from their sockets. Mason had spied what JV had: that Mama D'Lo's smooth, toned waist blended seamlessly not into legs but the scaly, muscled body of an enormous snake! Then, in an action so quick that JV was barely able to catch it all, Mama D'Lo leaned in as if for a kiss but

137

instead struck with lighting speed, winding herself around Stocky and completely wrapping him up in her tight coils.

JV's instincts yelled at him to snap out of his stupor and to run to the hunter's aid, but in a flash of movement and whirl of water, Mama D'Lo and Stocky disappeared into the stream. Mason pointed a trembling finger at the rippling surface. JV, aghast by what he had witnessed, grabbed Mason's arm and pulled the larger boy with him as he fled the terrible scene.

"Do you think she saw me? Is she going to...to get me next?" Mason's words came out in rasping breaths. JV shook his head as he ran.

"No. They promised. They promised that you will be safe."

"What if I tried to explain? Do you think they'd understand?"

"You could try, but it probably won't make much difference. They don't see things the way we do."

They kept running until, mentally and physically exhausted, JV came to a halt.

"Why are we stopping?" Mason asked, looking over his shoulder.

"We're here," JV replied.

Mason stepped into the clearing and looked about him. "JV, I don't see..." A gentle splash drew his eyes to the pond. Adelle stood at the edge, peering down at something.

For a moment, Mason simply stared. Then, in a whisper that swelled until it became a shout of joy, he repeated,

"Little Bird" over and over again as he ran toward his sister with arms outstretched.

Holding his breath, JV waited where he was. But both his hopes and heart began a rapid descent to the pit of his stomach when Adelle's face, now turned in their direction, failed to show any sign whatsoever that she recognised the young man racing toward her. She was still lost, and there was nothing more that he could do. Looking on, he saw Mason close the distance and sweep his little sister up in the air, squeezing her tiny frame against his chest. He was laughing, crying, and apologising all at once, seemingly either unaware or unconcerned that his hug was not being returned.

Then, as JV watched the bittersweet reunion, a brilliant shaft of afternoon sunlight suddenly bathed the siblings in its golden glow. Adelle rubbed her eyes and appeared to blink away her veil of drowsiness. Then she smiled and threw her arms around her brother's neck.

"Mason!" she squealed. "I had the best dream ever… even though it didn't start off that great. First there were these strange children who wanted to play, but they made me scared, and then I was with a beautiful princess who had lots of animals that needed taking care of, and she showed me how to look after them…and even taught me songs to help them heal. I remember one. Listen." She started to hum the sweet, melodic tune JV had heard the day before. "See?" she said after a few bars. "It was all so real, Mason. I wish you could've met the princess. She would've liked you."

"Oh, I hope not." Mason said, putting Adelle down gently. "Something tells me she wouldn't have been my type at all. Besides, the only person I'm happy to see right now is you, Little Bird." He hugged her tenderly again. "You don't know how happy. But come on. We need to get out of here. Just wait till Mummy and Daddy see you. They aren't going to believe it. Come on, JV."

JV glanced over his shoulder before replying. "In a minute. You two go ahead, and I'll catch up."

"You sure?" Mason's gaze flitted around the clearing.

JV nodded. Mason shrugged, started to leave with Adelle, then paused and looked back.

"Thanks, JV," he said. "She wouldn't be going home if it wasn't for you. And as for the other bad guys back there," he added, pointing in the direction of the hut, "their time is pretty much up."

Puzzled, JV was going to ask Mason what he meant, but the older boy stopped him.

"I can't tell you everything right now, but believe me. It'll all be over soon." Holding Adelle's hand, Mason left the clearing.

"So that's it?" JV asked aloud, turning around to face the trees. Almost immediately he heard the soft thud of hooves and then saw Papa Bois's form as it materialised from the green backdrop.

"Yes. All is once again as it should be, Man's child," the solemn Protector responded. "My charges have communicated to me their gratitude for what you have done, and Mama D'Lo and I also thank you for the role you played

140

in their rescue. You belong to a different world, Man's child, but should our realms ever cross again, know that from this day on you have faithful friends in the forest."

Humbled, JV gave a shy smile and nod of acknowledgement. There was much that he wished to understand about Oscuros, the Protectors, and their relationship with the animals and forest, but something more important begged to be learned, something that he had to ask while he still had the chance.

"Papa Bois?"

"Yes, Man's child?"

"Have you always been here?"

"As long as this forest has been, so have I."

"And you keep an eye on everything that happens?"

"If it has to do with this domain or my charges, yes. It is my duty."

"Well, did you happen to see...did you see who left me near the forest when I was a baby?"

Papa Bois was silent for a moment and then said, "I have always known who you were, Man's child: the little one brought to the edge of my domain by a Man's daughter whose face I did not see, but whose many embraces left wet stains on your cheeks before she departed. It was not my duty to do so, but I watched over you that night until you were found. I knew then, as I do now, that you are special, Man's child."

JV's pulse thumped. "And did she say anything? The woman who left me. Anything at all?"

141

Again, Papa Bois paused. "Nothing but two whispered words, Man's child. 'Akin Dawar' is what she said in your ear."

"Akin Dawar?" JV repeated. The words meant nothing to him. "Are you sure?"

"It is what I heard, Man's child, and it means 'wandering hero' in one of Man's tongues. She whispered those words before placing this in the folds of cloth that covered you." Papa Bois tapped the ram's horn on his chest, caught the gold coin that rolled out, and offered it to JV.

JV examined the coin. He had never seen another like it. An ornate anchor, with a hole at the top of its shank, divided the face in two, separating a smooth left half from a rough right one. He turned the coin over. There was an anchor on that face as well, but the halves were inverted, with the smooth on the right and the rough on the left. "I don't understand, Papa Bois. What is this coin, and why did you have it?"

"It is not my custom to concern myself with the trinkets of your race, Man's child, but I have, throughout the ages, witnessed the misfortune that coins like this have brought upon those who bear them. I therefore took possession of yours to temporarily shield you from danger, and pledged to return it when I judged you better able to bear its burdens. I honour that pledge today, Man's child. You have proven yourself ready."

"Ready? Ready for what?"

But the Protector did not respond. He merely looked at JV and the coin, and then he disappeared—leaving JV with a head full of questions and concerns. Was it his mother whom Papa Bois had seen? Was Akin Dawar his real name? Would he really be in danger now that he had this coin? Exasperated by the lack of answers, he took a last look at the clearing then ran to catch up with Mason and Adelle.

Chapter 12

Reunions and Revelations

JV, Mason, and Adelle stepped out of the forest and onto the dirt track that would lead to their respective homes. But though their feet followed the same path, each mind seemed to be preoccupied with something different: Adelle was relating the events of her unusual dream, probably in an effort to pin down and lock away its fast-fading details; her brother's facial expressions, which alternated between elation and concern, led JV to assume that

Mason was not only anticipating his parents' joy upon seeing Adelle, but also contemplating his answers to the many questions they would have for him; and JV's own thoughts were with Papa Bois's revelations about his past, the strange coin that was now in his pants pocket, and the remaining traffickers who would surely be coming after them for revenge.

Notwithstanding such divergent trains of thought, the wandering minds were simultaneously reined in when the three children rounded the last curve. Instead of beholding the usual unrestricted view of the village, JV and the others saw quite a spectacle in the distance. Police vehicles were parked haphazardly, their red and blue lights flashing; most of Alcavere's population anxiously stood behind long, narrow stretches of plastic tape; and a few officers listened to radios that squawked over the excited buzz generated by the masses.

"I know news spreads like wildfire around here, but this is ridiculous," JV said. "How could they already know we've got Adelle?"

Mason smiled. "Remember what I told you, JV. It'll all be over soon."

JV had no idea what Mason was talking about. All he knew was that this wasn't going to be the quiet return that he had envisioned. Naturally, their presence was soon detected.

"Look! Ah seein' somethin'. Ah seein' somethin'!" Doris's voice shrieked from the thick crowd. The buzz intensified, and as the returning youths got closer, they

145

could hear her even more distinctly. "But wait. What is this I seein' here? That lookin' like Adelle. Bless my eyesight. Look! Look! It's Adelle with her brother and Miss B's boy. Somebody run and get Paulette and Earl. Quick, quick!"

The villagers pushed forward and, breaking the line of tape in their way, rushed ahead to meet the young-sters, fully surrounding them before long. There were cheers, tears, prayers of thanks, and questions of course: Where had Adelle been? How did they find her? When did Mason get back from Landing Town? Through it all, Mason held tightly to his sister's hand and said only that he was grateful for the concern but had to get Adelle home to their parents at once. Then JV heard his name. His full name.

"Jason! Jason Felix Theodore Valentine!"

Granny B appeared through the press of bodies, her face a portrait of worry that relaxed only when she reached his side. Grasping his wrist, she closed her eyes for a moment, mouthed a few inaudible words, and then gave his arm a squeeze—actions that were enough to commu-nicate to JV that she had been anxious but was happy to see him and thankful that he had returned unharmed.

"Well, plenty action goin' on in Alcavere today," Doris said, beaming. She was speaking loudly enough for all to hear. "First the police swoop in and tell us they're doing a sting operation 'cause something happenin' in the forest. Somethin' huge. They won't say what it is, mind you, but I happen to know it has to do with some smugglers who set up shop deep, deep inside Oscuros."

146

JV and Mason kept silent.

"Ah tellin' you," she went on, shaking her head, "criminals and hoodlums workin' right under our noses. Nowhere safe for decent people to live anymore."

Two officers who had been attempting to regain control of the situation began shepherding the mob.

"Move it, please," one of them ordered. "Move it. This area must be kept secure. Behind the vehicles. Keep moving, please."

Slowly, the horde shuffled back to its former position, and the officers replaced the police tape. Meanwhile, JV watched as Mason and Adelle tried to extricate themselves from the throng. They were making steady progress when the mass of bodies suddenly parted on either side of the siblings, and the boisterous chatter faded to low mutterings.

He saw Mason focus farther ahead. Mrs. De Couteau was supporting her frail husband, who shuffled along despite the agony that each step seemed to cause, and they were processing up the impromptu path toward their children. Lifting his sister, Mason ran forward. Seconds later, he put her in their open arms. Overwhelmed, Paulette and Earl clasped Adelle between them and the villagers closed in around the reunited family. JV could see no dry eyes. He knew that there wasn't a heart left untouched by the fierce yet tender display of love for the little girl whose homecoming had seemed an impossibility.

He smiled. Now if only the sting Doris had mentioned would be successful and Phipps and his cohorts could be brought to justice. If not, he and Granny B as well as the De Couteaus might very well have to go into hiding or at least be put under police protection. But before JV could get too swept up in his imaginings of life in a witness protection program, a ripple of excitement—just like the undulating waves that swelled and shimmied up the shores of Alcavere's beaches—surged through the crowd.

"Look!" Doris proclaimed. "Ah seein' somethin' else! More people comin' out of the forest."

JV directed his gaze to the path leading from Oscuros. Even with his hand shielding both eyes against the sun's glare, he found it hard to tell exactly how many figures were coming their way. Perhaps five…maybe six? He could sense mounting tension as the small, indistinct group trudged along. He felt as if the villagers were collectively holding their breath. All except Doris.

"They have them. They have the criminals. Look! You don't see? They have them!" She was jumping and pointing.

JV strained to see more clearly, and after a few moments of concentrated effort saw that she was correct. Of the six persons coming toward them, two were stumbling forward with hands cuffed behind their backs while the remaining four provided a tight escort on the sides and to the rear.

Uh-oh, JV thought. *Only two? That means they didn't catch them all. Someone's missing!*

"And look, look, look!" Doris was screaming now. "It's Tricky Dixon! See him? On the left. Not the one fallin' down like an empty sack that they have to keep proppin' up, the other one."

Her notoriously keen eyesight clearly had the rest of them at a disadvantage. But JV could make out enough to tell that the tottering individual was Cutlass—still a little worse for wear due to the tranquillizers—and that the other guy whom she had recognised as Tricky Dixon was the boss, Migraine. JV couldn't believe it! To think that he had known where the fugitive was all this time.

"Ah told all yuh," Doris said smugly. "Ah told all yuh that Oscuros would be a perfect hideout for him." She promptly started to give an account of where she had been and what she was doing when the news broke about Tricky's escape, her early predictions regarding his where-abouts, the havoc he had probably wreaked while he was on the run, and the mistakes he must have made that led to his capture.

The monologue went on and on, but most of what she said washed right over JV. He was thinking, *If Migraine is Tricky Dixon, and the other captive is Cutlass, then where is Phipps? Hiding and biding his time until he can take care of any loose ends? Such as a twelve-year-old boy who knows too much?* JV gulped. Evidently it was time to tell the officers everything he had learned about the traffickers and their operation.

"I'll be right back, Granny," he said, trying to shake free of her grip. "I have some information for the police."

"Oh, you do? Well I'll be coming too." She kept hold of his wrist. JV didn't protest. She needed to hear what he had to say anyhow.

149

Inching along, they gradually made it to the plastic tape.

"Excuse me, ma'am," JV said, trying to get the attention of the closest officer. "Excuse me." But the policewoman wasn't looking in his direction, and JV's calls went unheard against the noisy background.

"Well, what about Mr. Phipps?" Granny B asked after his fourth attempt. "Remember him? Maybe he can help."

JV froze and his heart raced.

"Mr. Phipps?" he asked, horror-struck.

"Yes. Never thought I'd be seeing him again, but he's right over there." She pointed at the group of six that was nearing the first vehicle. "It's good to see that he's all right."

If JV hadn't been as rattled as he was, he would have certainly laughed at Granny B's naïve concern for their nemesis. In his current frame of mind, however, all he could do was cross his fingers and hope that he hadn't already been spied.

Reluctantly, he sneaked a peek at the persons beyond the tape and his stomach immediately did a somersault. Granny B wasn't mistaken. Phipps was among those who had emerged from the forest. But why were his hands free? Why wasn't he bound like the other two? JV almost raised a cry of alarm but then saw Phipps jovially punch one of the plain clothes officers on the shoulder and give the other two a thumbs-up, and he understood. Phipps was an undercover agent.

Stunned, JV watched as Phipps escorted Cutlass and Dixon to the back seats of separate vehicles. Phipps then looked up to scan the faces behind the plastic tape. His eyes rested awhile on the De Couteau family, but on seeing JV and Granny B, he waved and headed over to them.

"Mr. Phipps," Granny B said once he was standing directly before her. "I take it you weren't just passing through Alcavere after all?"

"That's correct, Miss B," he admitted. "Sorry I wasn't upfront with you, but I couldn't risk blowing my cover."

"I can understand that, son. Jason here actually has some information for you."

"Does he, now?" Mr. Phipps asked, studying JV. "Would it by any chance have to do with how hundreds of animals that were primary evidence in this matter happened to escape from their cages?"

JV didn't know what to say.

"Well, speak up, Jason!" Granny B commanded, elbowing him in the ribs.

"No...not really," he replied. "I thought one of the traffickers had gotten away, but it seems like you caught them all."

"Actually, there's one more who hasn't been accounted for," Phipps said. "Nathan Greene, the snake hunter. We would question Dixon but he's useless at the moment—he's been completely unresponsive since we found him wandering through the forest. He'll be sent to St. Maurus for evaluation—but I am hoping a certain other person can shed some light on what may have happened to Greene." He looked across at Mason, and JV felt imme-

151

diate concern for the older boy. He had no idea if Mason would tell Phipps about Stocky's demise.

"What's going to happen to Mason? He didn't know he'd be helping them smuggle animals. He was only trying to make some money for his sick father. And he helped me—" JV caught himself just in time. He had been about to admit to freeing the animals.

"He helped you what?" Phipps asked.

"Helped me find Adelle."

"Ah," Phipps nodded. "Well, don't worry about Mason. He was very helpful during the investigation. You see, after Dixon threatened to hurt his family if he didn't follow through with their plan, I told him about the undercover operation and asked him to go along with it. Your friend was very brave. He was my eyes and ears when I wasn't around."

JV remembered what Mason had told him back at the hut. That it was JV who didn't understand, and that things were more complicated than he knew. JV smiled. Mason was a hero, and so was he, JV. He knew he would no longer shy away from joining Mason and the older students on the football field.

"So what happens if you can't find Greene?" JV asked.

"The case is pretty solid, with or without him," Phipps said. "Despite the missing animals, we have my testimony, Mason's, and that of the remaining trafficker, as well as Dixon's handwritten list of buyers that was still on him when we picked him up. With that key piece, we'll be able to coordinate with international authorities and at least put a dent in this animal smuggling business. Plus," he added with a smirk, "I'm sure we'll have your cooperation, Jason, if you were called upon to testify."

"Anything I can do to help." JV wondered how much he'd have to divulge if they did in fact put him on the stand. How exactly would a judge react to testimony that involved Papa Bois, Mama D'Lo, and an unbreakable vow to free confined animals? *Probably not too well,* he thought.

"Oh, and just so you know," Phipps said to Granny B, "you were right about Jason. I had my doubts, but it turns out there really isn't too much he can't handle in that forest."

JV thought he saw a flicker of pride cross Granny B's face. But she merely nodded and advised Phipps to change his bandage every once in a while. Phipps in turn smiled broadly and promised he would.

"Well, if you two will excuse me," he said, taking another look toward Mason, "I still have another stop to make." He patted JV on the shoulder, slipped under the tape, and was soon lost in a sea of celebrating villagers.

Granny B and JV watched him go and then turned back to see the two vehicles that held Cutlass and Dixon pull off.

"So there seems to be a lot you need to tell me, Jason," she eventually said.

"Much more than you'd ever guess."

JV thought back to his first exploratory mission into Oscuros barely a week before and everything that had happened since. Had he really met and formed an alliance with Papa Bois and Mama D'Lo, rescued all those animals, helped take down a band of criminals, and brought Adelle back to the village safe and sound? Oh, yes he had. He—JV a.k.a Jason Felix Theodore Valentine a.k.a…. What was it again? He fingered the ring in his pocket. Akin Dawar, the wandering hero—had really done that unbelievable stuff. Something told him that as far-fetched as it all sounded, none of it would come as a surprise to his granny.

"Well, I think it's about time we got home," Granny B abruptly announced, jolting him out of his reflections and prodding him along. "You've had a full day, need a meal and a bath—not necessarily in that order—and have a tale to tell an old woman who can't stay up as late as she used to. I'm sure we've seen all the action there's going to be out here for the day, but if anything else happens, you know Doris will gladly fill us in tomorrow."

JV and Granny B began picking their way through the crowd.

> "Bosse B, Bosse B,
> Curled over like the letter C…"

Two voices were chanting nearby.

"One minute, Granny," JV said as he halted and examined the faces around him.

> "Bosse B, Bosse B,
> If I run you never catchin' me!"

He saw the culprits—the eleven-year-old Tolbert twins—and they were getting ready to start up again. JV approached them.

"Please don't sing that," he said.

"Why not?" they asked in unison.

"Because it's not nice. How would you like it if someone sang about your buck teeth, Selwyn? Or your stick-out ears, Sharon? It would hurt. So don't sing about my Granny's back. And if you hear other people do it tell them to stop, OK?"

The twins nodded and slunk away. JV exhaled loudly and was about to rejoin Granny B when a high-pitched scream, swiftly followed by numerous children's squeals of delight, signalled that there was yet another disturbance somewhere behind him. Snapping around, he nearly passed out from fright when a flying mass making straight for his head veered left at the last possible second and landed squarely on his shoulder. Then, in the midst of his terror, playful chants of "Monkey! Monkey!" sprang up around him. Gradually, he realised that there was nothing to fear, and reaching up, he exhaled in relief when his fingers brushed against Curty's silky fur.

"Hey, buddy! Didn't know I'd be seeing you again so soon. Thought you'd be swinging through the trees and enjoying your freedom right about now."

The capuchin gave JV a tug on the ear and slung an arm around his neck as if to say that he was quite comfortable where he was, thank you very much. The village children were soon crowding around, trying to pet the curious little monkey, and Curty was a good enough sport to let some of them do so. Pascal was one of those lucky few.

"Ith he yourth?" he asked, tickling Curty's feet. "Doeth he have a name?"

155

"He's a friend," JV responded, happy to see the younger Pearson again. His last visit to their house had seemed like ages ago. "And yeah...I call him Curty."

"Cool," Carol said, stepping forward. Unlike her brother, however, she showed no interest in petting the monkey. She was fidgety and appeared a little uncomfortable. Not exactly like herself.

"Everything all right, Carol?" JV asked, slightly alarmed.

"Um, yes," she said quickly. "I just wanted to tell you something."

JV's insides tightened. "Sure."

"Well, I know when I saw you...when you came to the house...I said you should stay away from Oscuros. Well...I'm glad you didn't. I mean, I had a really good reason to warn you—and I still need to talk to you about that, and very soon—but, anyhow, what I'm trying to say is, it's a good thing you went back in 'cause you found Adelle." She bit her lip and looked away. "I know how horrible it must've been for her to be lost and all alone in that forest. It's a scary place."

For the second time that evening, JV didn't know what to say so he simply stretched his arms out and gave her a hug.

"I know you were just concerned," he said stepping back, feeling slightly self-conscious. "You didn't want me to bump into the same stuff that you and Pascal did."

Shocked, Carol blinked and scrutinised his expression for any sign of teasing. There was none.

Lowering his voice, JV continued. "Don't worry, I know all about the douens. You won't believe the stuff I've seen or who I've met or…actually, maybe you will." He smiled.

Perhaps it was Carol's obvious relief or the big hug she gave him, but JV sensed the stirring of an unfamiliar though not unwelcome feeling. He added it to his mental list of good things to happen for the day. A light tap on his arm from Granny B then reminded him that it was time to go, and so, with a wave to Carol and Pascal and a promise to see them soon, he, Curty, and Granny B left for home.

❋❋❋

Granny B pushed open the door to the small brick cottage, and the trio entered. The setting sun had already sneaked in and left its gilded mark on the walls, hanging pictures, wooden floor, and everything else in its path. But though beautiful, the gold-tinged effect did not last long since, with a flick of a switch, incandescent bulbs blinked on, casting their own brand of light in the hallway.

With Curty still on his shoulder, JV followed Granny B to the kitchen and, leaning against the old refrigerator, thought how good it was to be back in his favourite room where everything was exactly as he had left it that morning. It seemed silly, now that he was in the safety of this beloved and familiar place, but there were times when he had wondered if he would ever see those grey linoleum tiles again, or the flour-speckled counters, or even Granny B, and he couldn't help but cherish how comforting it was to return to the simple life that they shared. A simple life that he had a feeling was about to change. He put his hand in his pocket and felt the coin Papa Bois had given to him. Would Granny B be able to tell him anything about it? He decided that he would show it to her and share everything Papa Bois had told him. But later. The past was not going anywhere. The present was what he had now.

Pleased with his philosophising, he looked up and caught Granny B as her astute gaze went from his face to linger for a while on the docile capuchin on his shoulder. He then watched her shuffle over to the cage by the open window and pause for a fraction of a second before unlatching the tiny door and leaving it to stand ajar. Kockot, who was on her perch pecking at something under a wing, fluttered down and hopped forward.

Granny B turned her back and headed to the stove. "Oh. Just one thing before you go to bathe, Jason," she said, adding salt to the contents of a bubbling pot. "Doris is going to need some help painting her house this vacation and I told her you have lots of time to lend a hand."

Nudging the door open a little wider with her beak, Kockot poked an inquisitive head out and looked this way and that.

"Huh?" JV asked. He couldn't have heard right. "What's that, Granny?"

"Boy, like your ears are worse than mine! You. Doris. Paint. Her house. Starting next week."

"But Granny," JV groaned. "Doris? Really? That's going to be pure torture. Why'd you do that to me?"

158

"Oh, what a question, Jason," Granny B said, her eyes still on the pot. "For passing the breadfruit tree, of course."

Kockot leaned forward and spread her wings.

GLOSSARY

Agouti

(Pronounced ah-goo-tee) A large, fast rodent that lives in the forest.

Alcavere

(Pronounced al-cah-veer) A small fictional village on a Caribbean island.

All yuh

You all.

Bachelor's button

A bushy herb that can be used in traditional medicinal treatments.

Bake

Similar to bread, but denser and made without yeast.

Bend de tree when it start to grow.

"Bend the tree when it starts to grow." It is best to mould children when they are young.

Better to mind old clothes than people business.

Even doing a nonsensical task is better than sticking your nose in other people's business.

Bosse back

(Pronounced bo-see) Bosse, which means hump in French, is used when referring to someone who has a hunched back.

Breadfruit

This large, prickly green pod has a fleshy interior that is edible when cooked. The leaves, flowers, and fruit of the breadfruit tree are used in traditional medicine.

Buljol

Flaked, salted cod that is fried with tomatoes, sweet peppers, and onions and normally eaten with bake.

Callaloo

A thick, soupy dish made from a dark-green leafy vegetable, okra, coconut milk, and seasonings.

Cassava

A root vegetable (also known as yucca or manioc)

Catch a vapse (to)

To act on an impulse or to do something suddenly or out of character.

Chadon beni

(Pronounced sha-doh beh-nee) A herb used to season meats and also used in traditional herbal remedies.

Coconut drop

A sweet, moist coconut treat.

Didn't say boo

Didn't say anything at all.

Douens

(Pronounced dwens) Spirits of children who have died and now roam the forests, wear straw hats, and have feet that point backward.

Duppy

A spirit, ghost.

Early o'clock

Early.

Eddo

A root vegetable that is only edible when cooked.

Elephant ear

A large, broad leaf that resembles the ear of an elephant.

Flambeau

(Pronounced flam-bo) A torch whose wick sits in a kerosene-filled glass bottle.

Bless meh eyesight!

"I can't believe my eyes!" This is usually said upon seeing someone you haven't seen in a long time.

Gundy

The large claw of a crab.

Heliconia

A tropical forest plant with bright-red, orange, or yellow flowers.

Hog plum

A small, tropical yellow fruit.

Hot foot

Said of someone who is always on the move, who is always out and about.

It takes two hands to clap.

Sometimes you need to work with others to get things done.

Jumbie

An evil spirit.

Jumbie bird

A type of owl whose screech means that someone nearby is going to die.

Kiskadee

A small yellow bird with brown wings and a black-and-white striped head. It is named after the sound of its call which, when heard, signals that rain is coming.

La Diablesse

(Pronounced la-ja-bless) A devil woman with a cloven hoof hidden beneath her long skirts and who wears a broad-brimmed hat to hide her glowing eyes.

Lagahoo

The equivalent of a werewolf, this shape-shifter often takes the form of a wolf.

163

Lantana

A type of shrub whose leaves are used in traditional herbal medicines.

Lime

To hang out with friends.

Mama D'Lo

Half woman, half snake, she protects the forests, its animals, rivers, and streams. D'Lo comes from the French phrase *de l'eau* which means of/from the water.

Mauby

Made from the bark of a tree, this drink is naturally very bitter and is sweetened with sugar.

Obeah

(Pronounced oh-bay-ah) Black magic.

Maxi taxi

A passenger van that is used for public transport.

One day for police, one day for thief.

Things may go your way one day, and someone else's way another day.

Oscuros

(Pronounced oh-scoo-rohs) The fictional dark and sinister forest situated on the outskirts of Alcavere.

Papa Bois

(Pronounced Papa Bwo-ah) Half man, half beast, he looks after the plants and animals of the forests. *Bois* is a French word that means wood.

Papaw balls

Round, green, sugary treats made from the papaya fruit.

Plantains

Similar to bananas, but bigger and usually cooked before eaten.

Provisions

The name given to root vegetables such as potatoes, yams, eddoes, and yucca.

Qualebay

(Pronounced kway-lay-bay) Said of something that is shrivelled or not in very good condition.

Saltfish

Salted cod.

Sapodilla

A round fruit with fuzzy brown skin.

Shining bush

A herb with heart-shaped green leaves that is used in traditional herbal remedies.

165

So-an'-so

"So-and-so" is often used instead of an uncomplimentary word when talking about someone. It is the equivalent of "you-know-what."

Soucouyant

(Pronounced soo-coo-yah) This old woman sheds her skin and turns into a ball of fire at night. Her fangs leave two small punctures where she has drunk her victim's blood.

Soursop

A large, prickly, green fruit, its sweet pulp is eaten or used to make drinks and ice cream, and its leaves are used in herbal medicines.

Steel pan

Also known as pan and steel drum, it is a percussion instrument traditionally made from empty steel oil drums that have been hammered and tuned.

Steups

(Pronounced sh-chups) A sound of exasperation or annoyance, it is made by using the sides of one's tongue to suck the back teeth.

Take in front (before in front take you).

Be proactive. Avoid potential problems by acting early.

Tamarind balls

A tangy, round, sugary treat made from tamarind.

There's more in the mortar than the pestle.

There is more to the situation than one thinks.

Toolum

A dark, round treat made from molasses and coconut.

Twef

A vine, the leaves of which are used in traditional herbal treatments and to protect against black magic.

Who sick does look for doctor.

If you're sick, you look for a doctor.

You couldn't catch me for dust.

This is an expression that describes how quickly someone runs. The person is running so fast that you would only see the dust they left behind.

The Author

Danielle Y. C. McClean is an author, a translator, an interpreter, and a teacher. She has degrees in French, Spanish, and law, and is passionate about language, mythology, and foreign cultures.

Photo by Jeff Tidwell

Originally from the Caribbean republic of Trinidad and Tobago, she currently lives in Tennessee with her husband and two children.

The Protectors' Pledge is McClean's debut novel and one of three winning titles of CODE's 2016 Burt Award for Caribbean Literature. You can visit her online at www.daniellemcclean.com.

CPSIA information can be obtained
at www.ICGtesting.com
Printed in the USA
FFOW05n1356260417